D0567031

	DATE DUE	
JAN 17 2006		
APR 0 2 2008		

PENGUIN BOOKS

THE LOVES OF FAUSTYNA

Nina FitzPatrick's first book, the story-collection *Fables of the Irish Intelligentsia*, won her—for a few days at least—the 1991 *Irish Times*/Aer Lingus Irish Literature Prize for Fiction. When this award was withdrawn after a dispute over citizenship, her name, her nationality, her sex, her number, and her very reality became a matter for fierce debate. *The Loves of Faustyna* can only intensify and complicate that debate still further.

NINA FITZPATRICK

The Loves of Faustyna

PENGUIN BOOKS

For Alodia, Wincenty and Mary E.

PENGUIN BOOKS

Published by the Penguin Group

Penguin Books USA Inc., 375 Hudson Street,
New York, New York 10014, U.S.A.

Penguin Books Ltd, 27 Wrights Lane, London W8 5TZ, England

Penguin Books Australia Ltd, Ringwood, Victoria, Australia

Penguin Books Canada Ltd, 10 Alcorn Avenue,
Toronto, Ontario, Canada M4V 3B2

Penguin Books (N.Z.) Ltd, 182–190 Wairau Road,
Auckland 10, New Zealand

Penguin Books Ltd, Registered Offices:
Harmondsworth, Middlesex, England

First published in Great Britain by Fourth Estate Limited 1994
First published in the United States of America in Penguin Books 1995

1 3 5 7 9 10 8 6 4 2

ISBN 0 14 02.4132 9
(CIP data available)

Printed in the United States of America

Contents

Contents

Prologue

In which there are Signs in Heaven

In the autumn of 1967 a cloud in the shape of human buttocks appeared over Kraków. Towards evening the cloud reddened and the angry rump drew more and more spectators into Mariacki Square. People pointed and laughed, but their jokes were tinged with unease. They were used to various signs in the heavens, such as the Virgin Mary, bulbous rosary beads, Marshal Piłsudski on a white horse and choirs of overfed angels. This, however, was quite unnatural. On previous occasions the sky had been serious and preoccupied with the best interests of our country, both national and spiritual. All of a sudden it had turned facetious and shamelessly taunted us with a pair of muscular haunches.

What could it mean? The weather forecaster at the end of the TV news could barely suppress a giggle when she mentioned the cloud. It was an uncommon, though not unprecedented, meteorological phenomenon – possibly caused by toxic emissions from Nowa Huta. Most certainly it would disappear overnight. Then gleefully: it was heading towards the east!

The following morning the cloud was still there, more luminous and compact than ever. It had a yellowish tinge and seemed about to discharge itself over the city. Krakovians on their way to work stood rooted to the ground. Some automatically opened their umbrellas though there was no hint of rain, others clustered in little groups to discuss the latest aerial developments. This time the jokes were fewer and people felt a little apprehensive, a little embarrassed. For how could you conduct your normal affairs in a normal way with a splendid yellow bottom displayed two hundred metres above your head? How could a boy say I love you to his girl in the presence of that ridiculous reminder of what, fundamentally, his love was all about? How could a procession of pilgrims heading for Jasna Góra go on with their Paters and Aves without falling into distraction and losing count? Weren't the party secretaries just a bit too literal when they claimed that the dark clouds hanging over our country were generated by imperialist and reactionary centres in West Germany and the USA? And what ran through the heads of the housewives as they stood for hours in queues for toilet-paper outside the *drogeries* that morning?

As the day wore on and the bottom in the sky failed to disappear, we were invaded by a vague sense of having committed some mortal sin which God was now bluntly pointing out to us. We had thought of ourselves as a Promethean tribe, the crucified nation of Europe, the Irish of the East, the last Mohicans. But no! There it was, all native depravity, all the sloth, filth and corruption finally exposed. Passers-by turned their heads in the street as if afraid to discover the truth in one another's eyes.

Only the radiosthetes were jubilant. Now they were sure that Father Klimuszko was on to something after all. Kraków was the seventh chakra of the earth. As such it was a place of subtle radiations and magnetic auras. They were all concentrated under the Wawel Castle. This remarkable fact had been mentioned in the prophecies of St Malachi and confirmed by a visiting Hindu professor. When evil stalked the land, the auras pulsed with intensified energy.

In the evening when the buttocks, as if tensing and straining, turned brick-red once more, a preacher with a wooden cross appeared in Floriańska Street. Godless atheists! Communist infidels! The Curse of St Stanislaus is upon you! That's what you get for harkening to the Evil One! That's what you get for turning your back on the Almighty! You've turned your back on Him and He's turning his back on you!

A policeman with the help of two friars from the Mariacki Cathedral briskly hauled him away. The idea that God was flashing his arse to show his displeasure with Kraków was too preposterous to be endorsed either by the secular or by the religious authorities of our city. Besides, what would the French tourists buying fake holy icons in the Linen Hall think?

When dusk fell and the infamous sight melted into the darkness everybody sighed with relief. But the talking and guessing went on far into the night. Would the buttocks return the next day? How long would they last? Was Kraków about to suffer the fate of Sodom and Gomorrah? And why Kraków and not Paris or New York?

(Or Dublin for that matter?)

Adventure One

In which Faustyna, Inspired by the Cloud, Arranges for her Defloration

'Why Kraków and not Paris or New York?' I asked Oblivia.

'I don't know,' she giggled. 'It's the finest pair of buttocks I've seen in a long time. It reminds me of Antoni.'

We were leaning on the windowsill watching the apparition fade into the night sky. Our room was on the tenth and most dangerous floor of the student hostel. Everybody knew that the tenth floor was radioactive and that it was held together by a collective belief that it would not collapse just yet. Were it to collapse it would crush six hundred and fifty girls sprawled on rickety divans below it and finally ravage the thousands of knickers that hung out to dry on lines over the bathtubs.

On the day the cloud appeared knickers became a favourite topic of conversation in the hostel. The whole building was giggling and guffawing. The approaching end of the world fired us with excitements that not even the concrete and asbestos could quench.

Oblivia was more in demand than ever. She spent the day rushing down to the phone in reception and finally landed herself with three simultaneous dates. I felt a sickened, resigned jealousy. If the end came tomorrow, I would perish pure as a parsnip.

'How will you manage?'

'I don't know,' she said absentmindedly, 'but since it may be the last time . . . '

She belonged to a special breed of women who answered 'I don't know' to most things. That's why everyone called her not Olivia but Oblivia. Rather than striving to produce an adequate response she would say 'I don't know' with so many different inflections, flavours and textures that most men found her disturbingly profound.

There was no trace of guilt, no sign of embarrassment in her admissions of ignorance. On the contrary, there was self-confidence, discreet allusion, reproach even. She I-don't-knowed herself into the third year of law studies without special difficulties. Her mysterious response made some of her examiners ashamed of their questions and others more aware of their manhood. By holding out an empty head and silence to them she forced men to fill the disquieting vacuum with their own ideas. They had to surpass themselves and were therefore grateful to her for their own brilliance. Her thoughtless emerald eyes, golden Byzantine complexion, brisk breasts and wasp waist turned men into a secret fraternity of voyeurs. To some unfortunates she became an addiction, a necessary void that vexed them into bad poetry.

I, by contrast, knew everything, remembered everything, had the facts beaten into me and nobody wrote a word in my praise.

◊

It was through Oblivia that I came to understand the effect that women have on world affairs. As it happened, she was to miss her appointment with history. Unwittingly, on the night of the buttocks, she passed it on to me.

'Look,' she said, pulling on her stockings. 'I have an idea. I take Mateusz, you take Mikhail Sergeyevich and we dump Jozek.'

'Wait a minute! What Mikhail? I'm not going anywhere.'

'Don't make unnecessary difficulties. If you don't go he'll be very disappointed.'

'But it's you who have the date, not me.'

'He's never seen me, I've never seen him, so there's no problem. You go there, you drink a cup of tea, you talk about, I don't know, Pushkin or something like that. Besides, you speak Russian better than I do.'

'A Russian?'

'Oh, don't panic. He's here with a delegation of lawyers from Irkutsk or Mlynsk or, oh, I don't know. A friend gave him my number. Besides, don't tell me that you're going to sit here all by yourself while everybody else goes *balanga*.'

She whirled towards the door in a blizzard of scent.

'The Europa Hotel. Downstairs restaurant. At eight.'

'Wait. How will I know him?'

'Oh yes. He says he looks sad and wears a grey jacket.'

A Russian! I needed to analyse the situation. Let's take the cup of tea first. If a girl is invited to a man's place for tea she doesn't refuse. Why – is she afraid of something or what? If she refuses it can only mean that she has a sick imagination. I had often been for tea to men's places and nothing ever happened.

But what if something happens this time?

A Russian! My great-grandmother did what she could to the Russians under very unfavourable circumstances in the times of the Tzarat. On Fridays she would hire two half-starved Russian soldiers for a rouble each to play with her children. She would order the soldiers to stand in the middle of the drawing-room and then loose her offspring on them.

'Crush the Muscovites! Beat the shit out of them! Kill the bastards,' she screamed, shaking her fists.

And the children kicked and bit and beat the poor Sashas and Sergeys, who bore it calmly because it meant that their bellies would be full for another week. As for my great-grandmother, it was her small retribution for the hangings and the deportations and the broken backs in the Siberian mines. *My dear sons, I went to war, just as your Grandad went before, and Grandad's father and his grandfather, to fight the savage Russian foe.*

What if Mikhail son of Sergey son of Vanya had come for his revenge?

It couldn't be. We were now fraternal nations with clean blank pages in the history books in place of tales of ancient bestialities.

◊

I was a virgin but I had no illusions. I was the kind of woman who had to be ravished. I was so full of myself that I could never yield to anybody without being forced. I had to be taken against my will. I knew that in my case rape of one kind or another was a historical necessity.

Looked at this way, Mikhail Sergeyevich was a godsend. He had dropped out of the sky specially to . . . No, no, that was going too far. But if he wanted to ravish me then his role as an imperial Russian would give him that bit of extra jizz. On the other hand, the fact that he was a barbarian would take the sting out of it. He was the elemental, the irresistible power of flood and fire. He was fate. He had come to Kraków, he would do the necessary, ravage the ravageable and go.

It would all be over in one night and then, hail, rain or Apocalypse, I would at least die a woman.

And so, on the Night of the Cloud, I went to my deflowering in the Europa Hotel.

The hotel was illuminated for the occasion and there were elegiac flags of the Brotherly Nations hanging limply from the balconies. In the foyer I lost all my courage. Two whores on a time-fuse of peroxide, fishnet stockings and mini-skirts sizzled away in a corner and batted their thick eyelashes at me. One of them smiled.

I cast my eyes down on the carpet. But there was no refuge there. A large oval drink stain leered up at me like an addled vulva.

I couldn't go ahead with it. Back in the secure, radio-active rooms of our hostel it had seemed an alluring prospect. But now I was mortified by the shamelessness of my own scheming. If I lifted my eyes I would see that everybody knew. Such a decent girl! And just imagine – with a Bolshevik. As if those vampires hadn't drawn enough blood from the nation already.

Apocalypse or no, I couldn't do it.

A group of pregnant men in drip-dry shirts and nylon raincoats rotated towards the restaurant. They were like fat spinning-tops wobbling at the end of a spin, bumping into one another cheerfully, lifting up their bellies the way girls lift up their breasts. Their wives followed, wearing Crimplene dresses and loud smiles.

I slipped into the dining-room in the eddy of the wives and found myself a corner table where I could keep an eye on everybody.

The restaurant was full of tipsy Krakovians and tourists on a final spree before Cosmic Closing Time. They sang obscene songs, broke the bread of wisdom and shared the chalice of remembrance. A sour lava of smoke, steam and spittle billowed slowly from one corner of the room to the other. *We're a lava field, with surface cold and dirty, hard congealed, but there are fires beneath no years can end; let's spit on this foul crust and then descend.*

Our jaded national poems hang over me like a sentence.

◊

10

I heard the familiar, sweet–brutal sounds of Russian coming from a table near the door. Two men were quarrelling. The third sat bathed in coppery light, fingering his watch and staring down into the secret recesses of his Slavic soul. *These people's bodies like thick fabric which nests the wintering caterpillar soul . . .*

Mikhail Sergeyevich, I was sure of it. He was broad-faced, broad-shouldered and very sad. A girl in an evening dress entered the dining-room. Mikhail Sergeyevich's soul rose shimmering to his face – and sank back again as the girl called out raucously to her boyfriend at the bar. In that unguarded moment he emanated the boundless melancholy of the steppes and the birch groves and the viscid flesh of boletus. I could smell it in the dining-room air over the reek of cabbage and *pirogi*.

How could I go and introduce myself with Rosencrantz and Guildenstern leering in the background? They were drunk and they sniggered at Mikhail for wasting his best shirt on a Polish hussy. He bore their abuse nobly for a while, shaking his head and looking officiously at his watch. Finally, weary of their inanity and my absence, he got up and left the restaurant, dragging his soul at his heels.

I made up my mind. I would allow Mikhail Sergeyevich to deprive me of my virtue. Russian or no Russian he was a man with a soul.

'Are you looking for someone, miss?'

The receptionist swept me with his one eye from head to toe.

'Yes. I mean no. I just wanted to leave a message, that's all. I'll come tomorrow.'

'Hee hee, there might not be any tomorrow.'

'I'd forgotten.'

'Some cloud, what? As for myself I have survived three ends of the world. The First World War, the Soviet Revolution, the Second World War. Not bad going? And in the end this cloud will do for us!'

He leaned towards me, his breath stinking of Żubrówka.

'I'll tell you what it is. The Russians are testing a bomb. We're the guinea-pigs. That's what these bastards have come here for. They're here to test our reaction.'

'Why should they want to do anything like that?'

'Why? Because it's convenient. A little cloud will do the job for them. You need no army, no propaganda, no Jews, just a little cloud.'

No Jews. A familiar chill ran from my heart to my feet. Every time it descended, I descended too.

'Excuse me. What is the number of Mikhail Sergeyevich's room?'

The receptionist's face went pale but he stared at me with his unblinking brown eye.

'I have no such name.'

'Very well. What are the room numbers of the Russian lawyers? I have an appointment.'

I could hardly stand on my feet.

He hesitated for a moment and then gave me the numbers in a voice meant to exclude me from the land of the living.

I knocked twice on all the doors along the Russian corridor praying that nobody would answer. The radio was on and blasted soul-wringing songs through the walls. Like a dowser over a black spring I knew, my belly knew, when I stood outside Mikhail Sergeyevich's room.

I knocked again but he couldn't possibly hear me. My Guardian Angel was offering me every chance to retreat and flee the infamy. And yet I pounded on the door like a madwoman demanding defilement.

The songs came to an end but my resumed knocking was drowned out by the *News at Eight*. I opened the door and the imperialist war in Vietnam flooded out mixed with the scent of eucalyptus toothpaste.

Mikhail Sergeyevich in an unbuttoned pink shirt stood to attention beside the handbasin and smiled at me with a mouth full of foam.

'The radio!' I shouted, pointing at the loudspeaker. He shook his head and helplessly spread his hands. I understood. We had the same system in the student hostel: once on the radio couldn't be turned off by the residents.

I bowed a nervous, understanding bow. He bowed back to me, his smile widening. I bowed again, trying desperately to remember the Russian greeting which I had studied for thirteen years at school. And so we bowed back and forth like a pair of geese. We bowed and bowed until he burst out laughing. His gaiety carried me with him. Still chuckling he pointed to the sofa with his tooth-brush and returned to the handbasin to rinse out his mouth. He gargled and snorted and spat with great Russian fervour and satisfaction. He shivered and shuddered and threw cold water on his face.

I felt like a filly waiting for the stallion. His roguish smile when he turned to me again confirmed that he looked on the matter in much the same way himself.

He smiled gaily, as if the centuries of monstrosity that lay between us had never existed. Generations of his ancestors had followed the plough and slept in haylofts. The murder of millions had given him the chance to keep his hands soft and to strut around hotel rooms in foreign countries.

There was no conflict in him – with the world, with himself – no crack, no wound. Nothing blistered or bled in him, as it should.

A hatred, not my own, stirred in my belly. Great-grandmother shook her fist in my face and screamed. You slut! You Judas!

Very well, I'll have tea and I'll go.

We drank our tea philosophically, now and then nodding our heads as if to say: Isn't it a crazy old world we're living in? The radio gave out the high-water mark for all the major rivers in the country. Neither of us attempted to move beyond the preconceived idea we had of one another. We renounced without a qualm one another's geology. There were deep strata in both of us – Permian, Devonian, Silurian, Cambrian, Pre-Cambrian – which we tacitly agreed to leave unexplored. We stopped at the pencil-thin surface, the downs of the breast and haunches, the curve of the knee, the flare of the nostril.

I asked him for a cigarette but he misunderstood.

'Good,' he shouted against the radio, 'I see you don't like to waste time.'

And he grabbed our glasses and emptied them out of the window on top of the banner of the German Democratic Republic.

He's going to do it now, I thought in a panic, and stood up.

'Sit down, sit down!' he cried, and I sat down obediently.

'Now let's see what we have here,' he winked at me and pulled out a bottle of Kalinka from his suitcase.

I was relieved. Perhaps I'll get plastered quickly and feel nothing. But what if I don't? My anxiety, like a defence-less hairy moth, blustered round the room and bumped into everything. It blustered for a little while, poor thing, and then it stopped.

'To the friendship of the Polish and Russian people!' Mikhail Sergeyevich shouted and tossed back his vodka.

'Amen,' I said and followed suit. 'Amen.'

He refilled our glasses and looked at me encouragingly.

'To the Polish–Russian combine-harvester!' was the best I could manage.

He winked at me again and emptied his glass. I felt like crying. He was a stage Russian and I was a stage Pole and how could we possibly do it perched on such tall stilts?

'Do you want to see the town?' I shouted and stood up again in a last attempt to avert what was inevitable.

'But it's night! You can't see anything at night!' he shouted looking at my bosom. 'To peace!'

'And the dove!'

'To the ladies of Kraków!'

'And the gentlemen of Siberia!'

His brows shot up.

'And their Five Year Plan!'

I saw the confusion in his eyes as he struggled to find the proper reaction. Will he throw me out?

He burst out laughing. He laughed and shook his head in bewildered approval. Once again his soul soared up and my soul leapt in recognition. For a moment we were suspended above the maw of History, the rage of the poets, the graves of the martyrs and my great-grandmother's unforgiving face.

All I could think of was my underwear.

I had put on the matching set with the sunflower pattern which I usually wore when going to the doctor. They were a diversionary tactic intended to confuse an invader with their cheerful innocence. Only a brute would lay hands on such trusting, open-eyed blossoms.

Mikhail Sergeyevich was a brute. Or perhaps he understood that that was what was half-required of him. He shouted a militant *Na zdarovie*, emptied his glass and sat down beside me.

Now, I thought, and I saw the same word written in Cyrillic on his broad Slavic face. Now.

I felt his hand moving up and down my back and then unbuttoning my dress. He was blowing a mist of warm vodka across my cold shoulder-blades.

'Crush the Moscal!' screamed my great-grandmother. 'Pluck out his eyes!'

I shrank into my sunflowers and they came off all the more easily.

Of course I could scream but I didn't. Of course I could fight but I didn't. I let him go on, aware that the whole thing was both necessary and ridiculous. The radio was broadcasting a repeat of a programme called *The Matysiaks Family*. My mother and I used to listen to the Matysiaks every Saturday evening. She was listening to it now. She was sitting in her matronly chair beside the radio, nodding her head and painting her fingernails. While she nodded away Mikhail Sergeyevich butted me triumphantly into a corner of the sofa. Just at the moment when Mrs Matysiak was scolding her son for escaping from reality and my mother was blowing on her nails he collapsed beside me, his face red as a bortsch soup.

No magic casements had opened on the foam of fairy lands

forlorn. No sun of liberation. Nor was my body temperature any the higher. To tell the truth, Mikhail Sergeyevich hadn't noticed that it was my first time and I had hardly noticed myself.

So, had I lost my virginity or not?

A disquieting thought, at first a little foul and hysterical, but then more and more confident and triumphant, filled my mind. I hadn't lost anything. If anybody had lost anything it was the Russian. After all, he had emptied himself with a howl into me and not me into him. He lay there unmanned and deseeded while I was ready to run to Planty Park and back. And how could anyone claim he had possessed me? What there was to possess, cuckoo spittle and snail slime, was inside me.

I put on my dress and left the room without a word. Mrs Matysiak was frying sausages for her husband. I felt a great tide of affection for her. I was back with my own people.

I ran through the miserly darkness of the People's Republic along an avenue of asphyxiated aspens. I ran over the dead leaves in the acid frost of the October night. The city exuded a discreet smell of decay, a dignified odour of decomposing monuments: Romanesque, Gothic, Renaissance, Baroque, Classical and Romantic.

And socialist realist.

I thought about my bum and the celestial bum in the sky. I could sense the cloud hovering reassuringly above me in the darkness. For a moment I was a part of the Great Chain of Being.

I tried to remember Mikhail Sergeyevich's face. Hard as I tried I just couldn't call it up. Even today, however often I see that face on the TV screen, I can't be sure.

For me Mikhail Sergeyevich, the man destined to destroy the Empire and to lead us all back to the nineteenth century, remains a headless horseman that rode me to nowhere.

Adventure Two

In which Faustyna Explains her Idea of Love and Prepares a Kamikaze Salad

Next morning, to everybody's relief and vexation, the buttocks disappeared. Rain fell and the Sunday sky was once again grey and dirty as a sow's back. We returned to normal, to building the ruins of a radiant future, ten years ahead of everybody else.

I was reading on the divan. Now and then I tore myself from the pythonic coils of Proust to marvel at how quickly I had recovered from the loss of, well, innocence.

On the other divan sat Oblivia, unwrapping a green dinosaur. It had a long fleshy tongue, and 'Kiss Me, I'm Irish' scrawled across its scaly chest.

(Go on, pull the other one.)

Above Oblivia's bed there was a shelf. It swarmed with porcelain milkmaids and cats with elongated ears, red-and-yellow dappled cows, clapperless bells, a fake bronze Eiffel Tower, wiry butterflies, wax roses, liquorice tarantula spiders, pink pompons and a fresh-faced John Lennon.

It was Oblivia's altar to the Goddess of Kitsch.

◊

There were hundreds of such altars in the hostel. Even our murderous history had failed to eradicate the primeval she-magpie instinct to accumulate junk.

The size of our cubicle was eight steps by four steps so I was sentenced to endure Oblivia's shrine. Worse, I knew her collection could only grow and grow. Once such a menagerie begins to spawn, everybody feels compelled to feed the brood of monsters.

I fed it too. I bought her a do-it-yourself crucifix for Coalminers' Day.

Sometimes, when I had drunk too much bison vodka before going to sleep, a dappled cow bore the cross back to me, the tarantula, pink pompons, milkmaids, butterflies and dinosaurs marched across my breast and up my throat and over my face. As I tore them off gobs of flesh came with them. Gasping for air through the swarming trash I ran to the door but it was always locked.

Enough, I said to myself a thousand times. I'm getting out of here.

Which I did, in my head.

Laboriously Oblivia twisted up the tail of her dinosaur into a question mark.

'Tell me. How did it go with the Russian?'

'So so.'

'Did you have a smooth landing?'

'Please. Do you mind?'

But my ferocious return to Proust only riled her the more.

'Are you going to read yourself rancid after your first fall?'

'How do you know it was a fall?'

I was going red. She gave me a knowing smile.

'Mikhail Sergeyevich has been on the phone again. He said I left, I mean you left, an intimate garment in his room. "*Intimnaya garderoba*", he said. I'm not sure about the rest. I think he asked me if he could keep it as a memento or should he send it back.'

I felt as helpless as a turtle turned over on its shell.

'It had a sunflower pattern,' Oblivia went on mercilessly. 'Big yellow flowers that follow the sun. This-a-way in the morning, that-a-way in the evening,' she swayed her head.

My puny turtle limbs beat the air, all the tender parts exposed.

'Come on, you've joined the human race at last. Look at me. I'm twenty-three and I've had sixteen lovers and two abortions.'

Oblivia had reached the stage where sixteen lovers and two abortions were mere words to her. For me words were still physical and intrusive. They smelled and groped, they dazzled or deadened me. On previous occasions when she boasted about her affairs, her stories took flesh before my eyes. Sixteen hairy bodies thrust at her and ejaculated into her belly. Blood-stained foetuses spilled out of her womb.

This time the bodies seemed less corporeal. I had begun to pass the threshold where the actual experience of things dulls the experience of words. Soon I would no longer flinch from 'make love' or 'sperm' or 'state enemy' or 'gas chamber'. Nor would I any longer be able to bury my nose in the echoing vesicles of Con-ne-ma-ra or Ma-da-ga-scar. Their magic would dissipate like the importunate cloud over Kraków.

Stealthily Oblivia slipped off her shoe, took aim and flung it at a pair of cockroaches that had crept out from under the sink. Then she lit a cigarette and swayed her hips into the divan beside me.

'So now you've been undressed by a man. That's a start anyway. If you fell in love you would become completely normal.'

'What do you mean normal?'

'Look at you. Stiff as a board.'

She ran her hand down my back.

'God but you're stiff. You should be stroked regularly. You're getting all stringy and salty with those books of yours. A regular lover would fluff you out a bit.'

She looked at me closely.

'Are you up to it at all?'

Suddenly I was awash with self-pity. I remembered the countless evenings I had spent sitting on the carpet in the corridor or freezing on the bench by the Vistula waiting for Oblivia to have her fill with her lover. While I froze I cursed her and I admired her. Her trysts were simple and lighthearted as the mating of butterflies in the summer. A young man comes, she twitters, he retorts, she giggles, he takes off her blouse, more giggles, off with her panties, she pleads in vain. Then thump thump thump, the divan will never stand it, do you have a cigarette? Oh God.

Why couldn't I?

Because for me falling in love was not just a practical problem. It was a labyrinthine undertaking of baroque proportions, the result of a disastrous misunderstanding.

My idea of love came from Marcel Proust. It went like this:

Countess So-and-So, borne on the currents of the gentle night, goes to a reception in the Faubourg St Germain. Her eyes shine like wet silica. The pink of her silk dress is more exquisite than the September sky above the Bois de Boulogne. In the drawing-room the air is transparent and congealed like an immaterial agate lined with the scent of musk and vanilla. She approaches Prince So-and-So. She knows that he has power over her. She wants him to want her. He too wants her to want him, even though he knows that he is about to get rid of her. Her heart, less resilient than of old, can endure the anguish no longer. She whispers: Our life together has become impossible. I leave you with the better part of myself.

It is a blow to the heart of the Prince. He wanted to retain the initiative of their parting but she has outmanoeuvred him.

And so on and so on.

Just as newly hatched goslings and chickens follow the first thing that moves so I latched on to the first book that moved me. It was *Remembrance of Things Past*.

The only way to handle love was to be on your guard at all times. Always stay one move ahead of the one you love. Never cease plotting and pretending. Always brace yourself for a disaster and have an escape route ready.

Years and years later I read a biography of Marcel Proust and learned to my astonishment that he was homosexual. Only then did I grasp the source of his anguish. All the women in *Remembrance* were really men in disguise.

When I made this discovery I felt cheated beyond all hope of recompense. Hard as I tried to read Lady Morgan's *The Wild Irish Girl* as an antidote, it was too late. The damage was done. To this day I haven't forgiven the French bastard.

Sartre is another one.

And Marguerite Duras.

There should be a Nuremberg Trial for writers who lead innocent people into misery and despair and wreck their lives.

Oblivia was excited by my incompetence and half-willingness to learn. Now that I had passed the first threshold she thought it her mission to push me further into the wilderness and see what happened.

'There's an engineer's party tonight,' she said. 'I want to introduce you to Jan.'

'No.'

'He's tall, he's got money, he's got his own apartment and he's just bust up with his girlfriend!'

My desire to withdraw to Combray fought with the compulsion to find out more about men and women and what they actually do to one another.

'What do I say to him?'

'You don't say anything. And you don't make smart remarks either. And you don't smoke. You just put on your plum dress and my cherry lipstick, he falls for you, he suggests you move out to his place and we all live happily ever after.'

◆

He stood in an embrasure at the engineer's party looking disdainfully at the blotched window-panes.

'Why aren't there any curtains here? Surely they make enough money on booze to invest in curtains?'

His body had an astronautical quality. Tall and lithe he was sheathed in what looked to me like a grey flying suit. His head was pear-shaped, with heavy lidded eyes, the hair on his skull a faint transparent stubble.

That's power, I thought. That's command and control.

Power shimmered around Jan like the nimbus of static electricity around space travellers in old science-fiction films. I could scarcely concentrate on what he was saying. An archaic female urge possessed me. I wanted to faint into him, helplessly, and leave the rest to providence.

While I was fainting away he talked and talked about curtains. When he took over as the director of his Institute the first thing he did was to install curtains in everybody's room. All his subordinates had to have curtains on their windows, even if they had to pay for them themselves. He used all his power and influence to get the best material. Curtains everywhere. A true sign of civilization.

I hardly spoke to him. I hardly thought about what he was saying. There are times when a woman shouldn't think or talk too much.

(Now you tell me!)

Like the princesses and princes of fairy tales who can only pursue one thing at a time – the waters of life, a golden rose, a cow with three horns – so I too could only pursue a single desire. I wanted Jan to want me.

It never entered my head that, besides loving and betraying, men snore and watch football and wear long johns in winter.

'You can't live in this syph,' said Jan when I opened the door of our room in the hostel and switched on the light. The cockroaches abandoned their frolics and ran back to the corner under the sink.

'You just can't live in this syph,' he repeated.

'We can if we do.'

Syph was an abbreviation of syphilis. Need I say more?

'No curtains,' I couldn't help remarking. 'But then we don't need any, do we, we are on the tenth – '

'Would you like to rent a room in my flat?' asked Jan abruptly. 'I mean, would you like to move into my place?'

His voice was a little shaky but determined.

I sank into the divan and felt the exhilaration of fulfilling my assigned role in the fairy tale conjured by Oblivia. I didn't need to plan or plot or outmanoeuvre Jan. He had cut through all my Proustian knots.

I hardly knew him but the princess who kissed her frog hardly knew the beast either. Were I to say no it would go against the etiquette of enchantment.

So I did it. I moved to Jan's place on the day after I had met him beside the curtainless window.

Exactly as Oblivia predicted.

We began with a sightseeing tour.

'This is my bedroom,' Jan announced triumphantly, like a bishop entering his cathedral. He drew back the drapes that hung around a heavy walnut bed.

I lie my cheek sweetly against the silken cheek of his pillow. My body, still remote after his embraces, slowly returns to me and composes itself into the ribs, knees and shoulder-blades that I know. I wake for short snatches to watch the drowsiness which lies heavily on my beloved. The faint light of dawn glows through the slits of the curtains and falls on the bowl of Bohemian glass, on the chimney-piece of Sienna marble. The servants will be about in a minute.

'And this is my kitchen.'

Reverently Jan approached a white press, parted the curtains of the tabernacle and took out an electric coffee maker. He held it up like a monstrance at Exposition of the Blessed Sacrament.

'One of the first in the country. I brought it from Munich.'

I tiptoe from the bedroom, my hair in a fiery fuzz, the air exuberant with the smell of mocha and warm rolls. The coffee-maker gurgles and cleans its throat happily on the . . .

'Now the salon.'

How can I resist a sideboard full of china and Waterford crystal, from which Madame de Villeparisis, Monsieur Legrandin and the Duc de Guermantes drink mulled claret on wintry days? Generals and academicians move to the orangery to continue their discussion of war and war's alarms.

Moving to Jan's apartment was a true initiation into womanhood.

There was a complete set of pink and gold china on his sideboard. It consisted of twelve matching plates, twelve cups and saucers, a sugar bowl, a jug and a tureen.

I almost cried when I saw it. I never had such a set. My mother never had one. We had drunk our tea and eaten our *bigos* from stray cups and plates that spoke of chance and chaos. Jan's china glazed me with a cool, tensile confidence; in touch with it I ceased to feel mediocre and mortal.

Everything went with everything else and there were no oddities. There were no buts or maybes, no will-hes or won't-hes, no can-hes or can't-hes. Jan's muscles too were well and truly honed for me, hard and practised in the arts of overwhelming.

My only obligation was to yield.

But how long can one remain overwhelmed? Or indeed be an overwhelmer? Just as middle-aged men who pull in their soft bellies in company can't keep them taut forever so I, after ten days of strained bewitchment, gradually lost hold of my Jan-shaped self. At first surreptitiously and then blatantly and in broad daylight, I relapsed back into sloppiness and psychology. I felt my father take possession of me again, that bundle of black rags on a sofa, chain-smoking and solving equations.

While I, to Jan's bewilderment, grew rank and weedy among my books so he, to my horror, grew grey and piscatorial.

Jan, as I came to realize, had a Janus face. His first face was alert and well-scrubbed and could even manage a beam of benevolent tolerance. If you caught it unawares, however, you saw the sleaze and slime rise to the surface and he turned on you the leery eye of an insecure carp.

Obsessively I brooded on the same question. Why could I no longer melt into him? Why did he relax into being a carp and I into a trollop?

At night when he reached out for me his fingers found a scarecrow and mine touched a fish. For a panicky moment I would feel the blood running cold in his veins and my nostrils filled with the saline smell of the sea. A gasping mouth gulped the air above me, a merman's tail thrashed my loins.

But he always managed to carry me with him through the surf, laying me, wet and pliant, under the blue plush drapes.

Fish or no fish, I couldn't resist Jan.

And yet I began to dread his homecomings. He would stand in the doorway, survey the room with a flat eye, noting the saucer, candlestick or eggcup I had used as an ashtray, the unwashed cup or half-eaten sandwich. Why weren't the newspapers folded away properly? Do we have to put up with your stockings decorating the arm-chair? How many times do I have to tell you to put the lid back on the jam jar?

He never said any of these things but I was only too eager to supply his recriminatory glances with a libretto drawn from my mother's reproaches.

Jan was a man of principle. He hated disorder. He abhorred the general chaos in the country. One day he said to me that all honest people should be given machine-guns for a few hours to wipe out all the crooks who were responsible for the mess. I don't think he was joking. If he was given a gun he would use it.

I tried to make up lost ground and join the ranks of those worthy of being given Kalashnikovs by telling him about my findings in neuropsychology and my exam results. I wanted desperately to spark some warmth or approval in his cold carp face. But his 'oh really?' made me regret that I had ever as much as passed an exam. There was irony, disbelief and pity in his eyes.

It wasn't that Jan wanted to destroy me. It wasn't that he was malign. He merely prevented things. He was St Jan the Thwarter.

Before meeting Jan I had been able to stand in queues for hours indifferently enough with an umbrella in one hand and *Totem and Taboo* in the other. Now I got testy and abused people whose faces I didn't like. I kicked young girls in the shins without the least provocation. I had a compulsion to write obscene remarks about my professors on the door of the student toilet. I became gluttonous. I smoked and cursed like a cart driver. Seven devils had settled in me: Rokita, son of Cunning; Boruta, son of Thuggery; Paskuda, son of Lust; Lelik, son of Sleaze; Frant, son of Treachery; Marcinek, son of Stupidity; Smetek, son of Doubt.

I waited a little until chaos was piled on chaos and my depravity shamed me into action. Then, one day, I sat on the unwashed floor of the living-room, lit a cigarette and asked myself what I should do.

Frankly, I had very little to offer as far as Jan was concerned. I was a pet parasite. I was pampered just so long as I didn't outgrow the host that fed me. But I would always be a potential threat to the peace, order and stability that reigned behind Jan's curtains.

Let's take a different tack then.

If ten million women of child-bearing age can be half-happy with their men with or without love, why can't I?

If ten million women of reasonable sanity can keep their apartments clean, why can't I?

Why should I live like a slut, why can't I have a normal life like everybody else? There was a man coming home who wanted his dinner in a tidy room and why shouldn't I prepare his dinner and clean up the fucking room and make him happy?

Yes, I'll do it for him, and what's more I'll do it voluntarily. Life, after all, forces us to perform many voluntary actions.

But it didn't turn out like that. A Big Nothing intervened. My great-grandmother used to say: there are Big Nothings and small nothings. A small nothing leads to ordinary everyday squabbles and misunderstandings. A lift goes out of order and wrecks everybody's day on the eighth floor. A Big Nothing is much more potent. It can destroy life and even lead to the ruin of a whole nation.

Cleopatra's nose, for example.

Or Hitler's testicle.

Or lettuce, in my case.

Apart from coming home to an immaculate apartment, Jan's dream was to have a green salad before dinner. He got this idea from watching American films where Bill and Mary-Lou began their meals with salad. That's how civilized people ate.

I must add here that at this time in our country lettuce in winter was as rare as a sane man in the west of Ireland.

(Oh, ho.)

So one Friday I didn't go to my neurotic personality lecture. I stayed at home and scrubbed the floors, washed the windows, cleaned the oven and removed spider-webs from corners with a broom. Then I went to the black market and queued up for two hours in an agreeable state of exaltation and moral fervour. When I finally got the lettuce I thought: if lettuce, why not veal?

So I joined the meat queue. The queue was short because the price of meat was astronomical and the stall-keeper had run out of wrapping paper. But this was no obstacle to a housewife possessed by a fundamentalist ardour.

I trotted home through the streets of Kraków with a kilo of bleeding flesh held aloft in my hand, like a marathon runner about to inaugurate a savage Olympics.

When Jan arrived I knew from his zipped-up face and clear brow that this time there was nothing to pick on and everything was shipshape. The floors shone, the sink sparkled and the piano bared its polished teeth.

Outside, in the streets, there were mountains of rubble, black reefs of mud, something dripped here, something rusted there, lumps of plaster fell from walls.

With us it was peace and porcelain.

Jan's eyes fell on the lettuce. He smiled. It was the

self-satisfied smile of a missionary who had converted a cannibal from eating his neighbours to eating the body and blood of Christ.

Outside, ex-human beings, hunters and gatherers of the industrial desert, shambled to their cubicles through the potholes and trenches.

We, lucky lovers, drew our chairs to the table and lit the candles.

I sat opposite Jan and watched him smile as he nibbled at his salad. The only sound that broke the sweet silence of reconciliation between us was the

patz

patz

patz

of the tap. Like most of the taps in Kraków, it couldn't be turned off completely, twist as one might.

Outside the night was smeared with tar. I could hear the first hysterical gasps of the Halniak wind blowing from the Tatras.

This is what being at home in the world means: Jan eating lettuce to his heart's content, me watching and the kindly tap going

patz

patz

patz

crexxx!

I cringed. I heard the dry sound of a tooth breaking.

Jan spat the tooth out and examined it with scientific curiosity. Then, with the same curiosity, he began to study the lettuce on his plate. He picked up a leaf and held it out to me without a word. There was little pocket of grit at the base of the stem.

He sighed. He shook his head. He took his plate and went to the sink. Scrupulously, he began to rinse the lettuce, leaf after leaf.

It wasn't the past that flashed before my eyes in an instant of time as I lay dying at Jan's mahogany table. It was the future. The desolation of post-salad days, of living on Jan's sufferance.

How would I ever face it?

Should I apologize?

Make a joke?

Start a row?

As my great-grandmother would say: there were two choices and neither of them good.

(This granny of yours is a pain in the neck.)

Jan finished rinsing the lettuce, sat down again and added some dressing.

'Well,' I said, shaking inside, 'our life together has become impossible. I'm leaving you – with the better part of myself.'

'Hmm. Is that because of the lettuce?' he asked with his mouth full.

'I'm leaving you this evening.'

'Who are you punishing now, me or yourself?'
'If you loved me, you would have eaten my salad, sand and all.'
'Why on earth should I eat unwashed lettuce?'
'If you loved me you would know.'

That same night I packed up my things and returned to my divan, like a beaten dog to his mat.

Adventure Three

In which Faustyna is Treated as the Tomb of the Unknown Soldier

I returned to my divan like a beaten dog to his mat. There were two thousand such divans in our hostel, all of them sodden with sobs and whimpers. I tried to heal myself with infusions of Guatama the Buddha: There is no such thing as I or mine. Cease to desire. Cease to want.

It was no good. It sounded too much like spilt communism.

I couldn't cease to desire. None of us could. No building in the whole of the People's Republic was so hollow with hankering, wanting, lusting and demanding as our dormitory.

When I left Jan I floundered into a great communal swamp of love rejected and scorned. You think you've touched bottom and then another depth gapes beneath you. And another. The whole hostel was sinking down, from one shoal to another, subsiding deeper and deeper into a pit of apathy where the cuntless babas awaited us.

I began to look at women who were well caressed through the glad eyes of men who would die for them.

When I gazed at Oblivia, at the exquisite amphora of her body, I could imagine the tortures of men who lusted to plant their seed in her.

While I studied her through men's eyes she twirled around in her new pleated skirt and flaunted her legs. Her shimmering nylons and high-heeled shoes detached themselves from her torso and slid out the window. They sped over Kraków like Chagall's lovers or those trees of dreaming whose fruit is the very eatage of forgetfulness.

'I'm off to a demonstration with Jurek,' she said. 'How do I look?'

'What demonstration?'

'God only knows. Something political.'

'Perhaps you should wear trousers then?'

'No. They said they need women so I'd better look like one.'

While Oblivia spent her afternoons demonstrating I tried to transform the salt of bitterness into the salt of wisdom. I took valerian drops, drank linden tea and redirected my hormones into my thesis.

I was studying absences and lapses. My subject was memory. The death of memory. I had set myself the task of exploring the degree of amnesia suffered by patients who had been operated on for brain tumours. My thesis was called 'Recollection and Recovery: a Study of Post-operational Traumas'.

I designed a test to be administered before and after brain operations. The test was to reveal by how much and in what specific areas oblivion had cratered the brain. For how long could memory hold out against the incessant advance of malignant cells?

There were problems. Nobody in the whole country had studied the struggle between memory and tumour. The Russians had worked on very selective cases, like soldiers with head wounds. Clinically the soldiers were much more appealing because a piece of shrapnel or a bullet tears out a definite area of the brain and leads to clear-cut impairments. But tumours are messy and wily and sly.

Professor Romanowski's brain, for example, was opened up three times. The first time, his mother and sons were removed; the second, the laws of physics and the titles of all his books. The third time, left–right, light–dark, tree–green, hurts–eats, all faded out. I held on to him as long as I could, both because I liked him when his head was full and because, as a matter of fact, he was my only long-term case. All the others died shortly after the operation.

The nurses said that as soon as a patient became my concern he was doomed.

In the evenings I returned from the neurological hospital and tried to sum up my meagre findings. Certain pages, elegant and well argued as they were, were so steeped in my rancid chemistry that I was ashamed to submit them. I could imagine my thesis supervisor sniffing at them in a state of disgust and arousal.

◊

My tortuous sublimations were interrupted one day by a knock on the door.

'Come in,' I said.

And He came in, hitting his head on the lintel.

For centuries I have been dreaming of this entrance and all women with me. Every detail was true to the ancient, bowel-blasting dream. Tall as a poplar, broad as a shield, fair as a parchment page, eyes blue as cornflowers, lips red as raspberries; how glorious the Sons of God when they take flesh and dwell among the daughters of men!

He had a bunch of red poppies in his hand.

Needless to say they were not for me.

He stood in the doorway, inclining his head, mute and beautiful.

'Oblivia, Olivia that is, is away at a demonstration,' I said in pain.

'I know, I just wanted to – it's her birthday.'

His eyes refused to meet mine.

'Do come in. Would you like some coffee?'

'No no no,' he blushed. 'I have to be going. It's just that it's her birthday. Will you take them?'

Awkwardly he handed me the flowers and turned to leave.

'Who shall I say? Does she know you?' I cried like a curlew.

'We are, I mean I am, you know, her brother.'

The incubus of jealousy let go of my bowels and I bid him farewell in a blissful stupor.

◊

Later that night, when I was already half-asleep, Oblivia tumbled in. As usual she barged open the door and switched on the light as if nobody mattered but herself.

'Swine!' she shouted, and again, looking around her triumphantly, 'Nazi swine!'

She came up to my divan. A noxious smell of onions had followed her into the room. Her eyes were red and watery.

'They gassed us and they beat us. Jurek is in jail.'

I got up and made her a cup of tea. I felt guilty about not endangering my life for whatever the cause was. But only a little. First I had to solve more urgent problems.

'Happy birthday,' I toasted Oblivia with my cup. 'Your brother brought you flowers.'

'Good God, I've completely forgotten.'

Suddenly she was stricken with grief.

'I don't have a private life any more.'

'For the last week there's been nothing but damn demonstrations. And damn debates. I don't count any more. Selfish bastard!'

She whined like a schoolgirl.

'Come on. Jurek's in prison.'

'Jail is too good for him. They're all a shower of bastards. None of them, not a single one of them, remembered.'

I let her cry to rid her eyes of the residue of the tear gas.

'Well. It's not that bad. After all, you've got flowers from your brother.'

But Oblivia cried even more.

'He rejected me as well.'

'Why didn't you tell me you had a brother?'

'Damian? Oh God, no. He's no use.'

'How no use?'

'He's absolutely no use whatsoever.'

'He's very beautiful.'

'It's all for nothing.'

'Is he – I mean, not interested in women?'

'No, no,' replied Oblivia and began to undress, still sobbing. 'I don't know. He always withdraws. He can't face it. He's very shy.'

'But he's utterly divine.'

'I don't know. He's blocked. He can't – '

'But why?'

I was more and more curious. Why he of all men? Why the poplar and the raspberries and the cornflowers?

'I don't know,' said Oblivia. 'You're the psychologist round here.'

'What about your parents?'

'They've always been very good to us.'

'Perhaps it's the mother?' I pressed.

'No. Besides she's ugly. Both our parents are ugly and healthy. Only we are beautiful and fucked up.'

'Perhaps it's you?'

'You mean he's in love with me?' Oblivia laughed bitterly. 'It's the other way round. I was crazy about him for four years. Four years – totally wasted. I wanted to follow him everywhere, even into the toilet. And then, when I proposed that we try it together – '

'You mean you proposed incest?'

'Incest? I don't know. That's just a word used to frighten people. I was in love with him, OK? He rejected me. I cried and cried outside his bedroom door. We were on holiday in Bulgaria. It was the worst time of my life. He was so . . . ' Oblivia was breathless. ' . . . beautiful that summer in his white shorts and blue T-shirt. With a white dove of peace.'

'Maybe he got shy because you kept after him so much?'

'I don't know. I think he was just born that way. He's always been shy and kind and he always brings people flowers.'

'But there must be some reason.'

'Oh, why does everything have to have a reason? Why is he shy and I'm not? Why am I stupid and you bright? Why do I look Icelandic and you, I don't know . . . '

'Jewish.'

'Sort of exotic, anyway. I didn't choose to be stupid or Icelandic. Jesus, this room smells like a pharmacy. What have you been dosing yourself with this time?'

'Mint. Valerian. Camomile. Salvia. Do you want some?'

'No. Look at these bruises! Nazi swine!'

While Oblivia wriggled in bed, sighing and sobbing to herself I chewed over what she had said. She had a point. Some things are as they are without rhyme or reason.

I wanted to dream of Damian. I invoked his face before I dropped off to sleep. But no. I could never dream of the man I was in love with. I returned, as I often did, to a primordial forest of gigantic horsetails and somnolent ferns.

The miracle happened on March 8, International Women's Day. Outside the door I found a bouquet of fresh freesias with a little note: 'To the girl with the flaming hair, Damian.'

I fed on the card for three days and wrote my thesis with the fury of a dishevelled romantic composer. I had only to glance at Damian's flowers and my flagging inspiration took wing. Everything took wing. I couldn't keep my eyes off her in whose eyebrows, lips and nose I found Damian. I went out of my way to make her laugh so as to see his mouth open to me. As usual, I went too far and Oblivia began to blush like her brother.

The signs were not good. Damian never came for coffee, never invited me to the cinema or took me to a ball. Instead he showered me with flowers. He left them on the divan when I wasn't in, hung them on the doorknob or entrusted them to the librarian. Most often he lay them reverently on the doorstep, as if our room was the Tomb of the Unknown Soldier. They were wrapped in foil and tied with a pink ribbon and accompanied by enigmatic quotations.

'Tell him to piss off,' said Oblivia. 'Those flowers of his give me a headache.'

'How? I can't even meet him for God's sake.'

'Well, then don't waste your time. I told you what he's like. There's nobody at home.'

So I did a daring and shameful thing. I hung a card on the door which said: 'I don't want your flowers, I want you.'

That brought a quick end to the flowers – and to the first part of my adventure with Damian.

♦

My defeat was full-blown and complete.

You stupid bitch. You should have held on a bit. You frightened him away with your bare-arsed lust.

But then if he can't take my lust he's not for me. If he can't come out from behind the poppies and freesias he's not for me. Whatever I do or don't do, isn't going to work.

My great-grandmother said: Even if you feed a cow with cocoa you won't get chocolate.

What was I to do with my bruised soul, so callously rejected by three men and so insipidly nourished on a tasteless diet of psychological research into the loss of memory?

Get rid of it! Exterminate the brute!

And so I did what generations of pissed-upon souls from Spartacus to Germaine Greer have done. I became a rebel.

Intermission One

In which the Red Dragon Eats Highly Intelligent Depilated Virgins

Krak (? – ?) the saviour of Kraków, became a rebel in spite of himself. By nature a rather shy and retiring man, he spent his days at a cluttered bench making shoes and galoshes for the belles of the city. Business was in decline. The Dragon who squatted in a stinking cave under the Wawel Castle had already devoured a large part of Krak's clientele.

As soon as a girl had her first period she was in imminent danger of being fed, along with half a dozen prime sheep, to the Dragon by the City Fathers. This was the only way to placate the beast and to prevent him destroying the city.

Over time the Dragon grew fastidious and his taste became more and more refined. He demanded spring lamb rather than old ewes or wethers and he established a set of aesthetic and intellectual criteria for the young ladies who were to gratify his palate. Then as now the classical Krakovian beauty was 165 centimetres tall, wore a 75B bra and spoke four languages. She had frizzy hair, a boyish body, an interestingly neurotic personality and she broke out in lurid beard rashes whenever she was kissed. In her heart of hearts she was a proper little bourgeois girl, snobbish but thankfully not too serious about herself.

The Dragon requisitioned only the most petite and intelligent girls with an IQ of at least 120 and no hair on their legs if you please.

As the Dragon's appetite grew there were fewer and fewer such beauties on the streets. The city, despite its elegant towers, elevations and fortifications, grew drab and graceless. You never heard laughter in Mariacki Square and there were no knots of schoolgirls exchanging obscene jokes under the arcades any more.

How long, oh Lord, how long, cried Krakovians deprived of their fairest daughters. Krak the Cobbler, who had no daughter but piles of unsold shoes, grew increasingly testy. He had scarcely made a pair of pompons for a young lady when she was carried off to the Dragon and naturally enough her parents would refuse to pay the bill. Trade in wool, sheepskins and glue was similarly depressed. Everything went to the Dragon.

When a delegation of City Fathers called on the beast to beg him to make some concessions (switching from girls to grannies for example) his red pot-belly trembled and he singed their beards with a raucous laugh. Gobshites, he said, I mean Comrades, as long as I protect your city from foreign invasion you have to pay the price. Sacrifices are required for future peace and prosperity.

Nobody had the stomach to raise the obvious questions: What foreign invasion? What prosperity?

The Fathers returned to the city, gingerly stroking the phantom limbs of their beards and wondering which foreign invader they could invite in to free them from their protector.

When Krak heard the tidings his patience snapped. I am a man of peace, he declared, but I like war. He organized a Defence Committee composed of the fathers of pre-pubescent girls and of shepherds who had a few hoggets left. Boys oh boys, he said, the devil with sacrifice. We must act now. Soon this God-forsaken city will become the saddest and most woebegone place on earth.

Amen to that! cried the Krakovians. Good man yourself! Down with the Dragon!

Hold on a minute, said Krak. It's not that easy. Militarily and logistically speaking, in men and matériel, we don't stand a snowball's chance in hell. We can only take him by subterfuge. I have a plan.

And so Krak disembowelled a lamb, filled it with sulphur and sent it along with five choice wethers and a distractingly beautiful, 165 centimetre tall girl with Tweety-Pie eyes to the Red Dragon.

With one lurid eye on the girl, whom he was saving for dessert, the Dragon lit into the lambs. When he swallowed the one stuffed with sulphur he let out a roar and galloped like mad to the River Vistula to quench his thirst.

Shite and onions! he railed as he plunged into the water, wind and piss! I spent the best forty years of me life protecting you and this is all the thanks I get!

He drank and drank until the river fell by two metres and then he burst. Chunks of gristle and marrow were found as far afield as Jastrzebie and Pszczyna. His free-range testicles ended up abandoned and unappreciated – and catalogued as fossilized cabbage heads – on a dusty shelf in the Department of Botany, University College Galway.

Bits of the Dragon's bones may still be seen hanging from chains over the Gothic door of the Wawel Cathedral. When the bones slip off the chains (*pace* Father Klimuszko) the end of the world is nigh.

(And what happened to the girl with the Tweety-Pie eyes?)
(You tell me. You're the one who's inventing things.)

Adventure Four

In which Faustyna Joins a Rebellion Against Herself

The rebellion I joined was badly timed. Our government, supported by leading Western intellectuals, had just announced that Eastern European standards of living and loving would soon overtake those in the West. The Iron Curtain would shortly operate in reverse to prevent Western workers becoming envious of the prosperity and emotional warmth of their socialist comrades. We were just on the point of making a leap forward. Of course we spoiled everything. Brother Russians had risked their lives, lost their finest sons to liberate us – and what did we do in return?

We were screaming, swearing and throwing stones at the statue of the honorary Russian Felix Dzerzhinsky and other national patriots. Thousands were milling around the Collegium Maius unaware of the prosperity that lay just around the corner of Kanonicza Street. Led by fire-brands, layabouts, gangsters, Freemasons, Trotskyites, teething revisionists, Zionist aggressors and Yapping Dobermanns of Imperialism they applauded a man who stood on a pyramid of tables and spoke through a megaphone.

This country is a parody of non-existent things!

Down with the Party! roared the crowd and I roared with it.

You can't play the song of freedom on the instrument of oppression!

Down! Down!

It's time to breathe, friends. Let the Party feel our breath on their backs!

Look out! Look out!

Two burly men in leather jackets grabbed the speaker from behind and rushed him off the tables.

He yielded to them with grace, blowing kisses to the ladies while the crowd booed and whistled. Another speaker climbed up the pyramid of tables and raised his fist.

Citizens! They will not beat us down!

No! No! roared the crowd and I roared with it.

We will multiply our thoughts to the point where there aren't enough policemen to control them!

We want freedom! We want freedom!

But there were enough policemen around to haul him down before he got any further.

Let me up, let me up! urged a man in blue jeans and a flamboyant orange scarf.

An El Greco Christ with wind in the hanks of his long hair. Our astral bodies tumbled like a garland of angels around him.

He stood on the tables with a bowl in one hand and a long straw in the other. He spoke softly.

Ladies and gentlemen. Listen to this!

He held up a plastic bowl.

The crowd fell silent.

Listen. This is what I have to say.

With a flourish he took the straw and immersed it in the bowl. A shimmering soap bubble rose into the air.

We watched its hesitant ascent in enchantment and cheered when it burst. Encouraged, he blew a swarm of iridescent bubbles over our heads.

Say it again! roared the crowd. Say it again!

A galaxy of scintillating bubbles hovered gaily over the steep roofs and pinnacles of the university. They teased us for a moment, turning and twirling as if uncertain whether to stay and play or climb higher, only to burst into nothing, as if they had never been blown into being.

Idiots! Don't listen to him!

A bearded man shook his fist over the crowd.

Can't you see he's confusing the issue? We need the truth and not bloody bubbles!

Shut up! Shut up, you old goat!

He's right! Let him go on!

There you are, brother Poles! jeered the bearded man. You prefer chimeras to the truth!

Get down, you old groucher! More bubbles!

No! Down with the bubbles!

Up with the bubbles!

Down with the bubbles!

Traitors, the lot of you!

The crowd divided into supporters of truth and supporters of bubbles. It was exhilarating: bubbles and truth fermented in me and my head was light and giddy. I felt as if I was to be the next speaker from the rickety tables. What to say to the people? What to promise?

'Faustyna, won't you join us?'

Tadeusz, who once taught me how to swim, approached with a banner. He leered.

Let me slow it all down. Let me get it as it really happened.

He comes up to me with a leer and a banner. He doesn't bother to conceal the leer.

'Are you able to hold this thing?'

One pole of the banner is impaled in me.

DOWN WITH THE OPPRESSORS OF NATIONAL CULTURE!

I'm embarrassed to be seen carrying it. I'm not used to such strong opinions.

'Fall in, everybody!'

A small procession forms behind us. So this is how you defend national culture and have the barbarians ride you down as you advance bare-breasted to the barricades.

'Down with the oppressors of national culture!' we chant.

I try it twice and then give up.

A second banner lurches into the square.

DOWN WITH THE PARTY BLOCKHEADS!

Placards of blockhead bosses, equipped with Hitler fringes and moustaches, bob into the square.

Then come the barbarians.

The clacking of their heavy boots on the living stones.

They encircle us.

Sons of bitches!

Whores!

Gestapo!

I'm caught in a vortex of hatred where we taunt one another through bespittled lips.

The riot police are pushing us against a wall under mullioned windows and gaping gargoyles. The bugler on Mariacki Tower plays his broken-backed call to hearten us and to announce that it's three o'clock. They will have to hack the flesh from my bones and break the knuckles of my fingers before I surrender this banner.

The enemy towers above me. I hardly feel the blow. My great-grandmother was right. Intellectuals are the *crème de la crème*. They are at their best when well whipped. I stand nobly erect for the next blow to fall on my defence-less shoulders.

'Stupid monkey!'

Somebody grabs me from behind and drags me away.

There is a flash of glasses, grim teeth and a shock of flaxen hair.

'There's no need to be so obliging, miss. Cut out the heroics, OK?'

I smile apologetically, he shakes his head and limps away. I'll never see him again.

I look around for Tadeusz but Tadeusz has disappeared. So I rush to the toilets in the student club. I want to see the noble bruise on my shoulder.

There are red and white leaflets on the washstand. At first I think they are about contraception and I start reading. But no. They say

MOSES GO HOME!

Why should Moses go home? And why in the toilet?

My heart begins to thump before the message hits me.

MOSES GO HOME!

Citizens! A foreign element is preying on the soul
of our nation. It is a putrid tumour. It rots
national culture from within.
DOWN WITH THE ZIONISTS!
DOWN WITH THE OPPRESSORS OF NATIONAL
CULTURE!

The eyes in the mirror staring out at me were like the fishpools in Heshbon by the gate of Bathrabbim. The nose as the tower of Lebanon which looketh towards Damascus. The head was like Carmel, and the hair like purple. Return, return, O Shulamite; return, return, that we may look upon thee.

The shoulder was bruised, black and blue.

◊

I walked down the stairs, forcing one leg to follow the other. I trembled and burned like a lamb branded for life. Return, return, Oh Shulamite, that we may look upon thee! After all, it's not every day that you take part in a demonstration against yourself.

'Faustyna!'

Below me on the stairs loomed a bunch of poppies with Damian attached. Awkwardly he climbed the stairs and halted a few steps below me. I couldn't raise my arm to accept the flowers, even if I wanted to. He blushed and cast down his cornflower eyes. For a moment neither of us knew what to do. Then he bowed as if to a statue and placed the poppies reverently at my feet.

And I, obligingly, turned to stone.

Adventure Five

In which Faustyna Almost Succeeds in the Art of Seduction while Perched on a Ladder

What associations do you have with the word 'locomotive'?

If you are smart-assed and have read enough bourgeois psychology perhaps you will say penis.

If you are a little less smart but tepidly imaginative perhaps you will say a monster or a dragon.

If you are a hard case perhaps you will say death.

All of these associations were marked 'problematic' in the key to my questionnaire. The best answer was: A locomotive is a locomotive. Or: With locomotive I associate a self-propelled engine driven by steam, electricity or diesel power for drawing carriages along railway tracks.

This answer was worth five points in the standard test for prospective train drivers. All of them had to pass a psychological test to find out if they were suitable for the job. I knew it was rubbish and they knew it was rubbish but they came to my office shaking with fear and laden with bribes. For my test was the last and highest hurdle on the way to every railwayman's nirvana. I administered the test scrupulously, asked all the necessary questions, checked reflexes and refused the bribes. In this way I became the most hated psychologist in the Psychotechnic Bureau at the Central Railway Station in Opole.

'So now, once again, what associations do you have with the word locomotive?'

The man opposite had dark hair and the pale long face of a chronic onanist. He looked nervously at the life-size semaphore beside me.

'Excuse me, Mrs doctor, but could I have a smoke?' He searched in his pockets for cigarettes.

'That's a hard one, now.'

'Very well, let's try again. When I say locomotive what pops into your head?'

His brow corrugated in an effort to find an answer that would please me.

'Well?'

'I give in,' he said heroically.

'What do you mean?'

'I don't know the answer, Mrs doctor.'

'Come on. If I say cat you think of . . . '

'Mouse?'

'Very good.'

He brightened up.

'If I say locomotive you think of . . . '

'Bicycle?'

'Very good. That's all for today. Why don't you take a seat in the waiting-room?'

He sighed with gratitude and bowed twice as he left the room.

I wrote under his application 'Recommended for post of driver with some minor reservations'. My other formula was 'Not recommended for post of driver but has good communication skills and therefore suitable for employment as conductor'. Out of every ten applicants I had to recommend two drivers, five conductors and three rejects. That was the quota. But sometimes there would be five drivers and no rejects and thus to balance the books I had to certify no drivers, no conductors and eight rejects out of the next bunch. The worst case was to discover ten able-bodied born drivers, no conductors and no rejects. When that happened I went sick for a few days and Barnaba took over.

Such was my work at the Psychotechnic Bureau at the Central Railway Station in Opole.

Opole was a mongrel city which suited my mongrel soul. Unlike Kraków, nothing there was firm or established or brought to completion: there were no pedigrees, traditions, curses or graces. Everything was possible there thanks to comrade Stalin. He settled Russians from Kiev among Lithuanians in Vilnius and Poles from Vilnius among Germans in Opole and Germans from Opole among Germans and Russians in Leipzig.

As a result everybody in Opole was hiding something: the Germans that they were still there, the Poles that they shouldn't be there and the Russians that they ran the place. The whole of Opole county was entirely confused and called 'The Recovered Land'. What was recovered was territory owned one thousand years ago by an ancient Slavic tribe called Polanie and to hell with the Germans who had dwelt there ever since.

I got to know the city very well because I was thrown out of one apartment after another for untidiness. Somehow I hastened the natural entropy of places. As soon as I took over an apartment unwashed dishes grew grey mould, mushrooms spawned in ashtrays, flowers and cats died of thirst and the plumbing convulsed with thrombosis. When I lived in the student houses there was sure to be some girl who was interested in objects and surfaces, concave and convex, and who kept them polished. In my company, things ceased to nag and demand and quickly degenerated into total indolence. A chair or a bed became senile after a few months, the lifespan of a cup was hardly more than a week.

So when one evening Mrs Drut and Mrs Huk (her witness) stormed into my room, looked around aghast and said just four words: Get out you slut, I packed up my bag without protest and left.

I stood outside the tenement house, lit a cigarette and asked myself what to do. Frankly, there weren't any more friends that would have me. The only place that would have me was the Psychotechnic Bureau at the Central Railway Station where I tested the railwaymen for their reflexes. There was an old couch in the waiting-room and a sofa in my office. There was a toilet and an electric plate for brewing coffee. I could imagine myself growing old there, entertaining famous artists as they passed through the station. No artistic career would be complete without stopping by Opole to see me on the way to higher achievement. I would be in all the memoirs.

So I went first to the Railway Station restaurant and ordered a huge cutlet and two glasses of *sliwowica* to celebrate my new life. Long past midnight, I turned the key in the door of the Psychotechnic Bureau which was to be my salon for the next sixty-plus years.

As soon as I opened the door I knew there was something wrong. There was an indefinite presence in the room, a smell or breath without substance. I hesitated for a moment whether to stay or to go but my nature is to dig deeper whatever hole I find myself in instead of climbing out. So I groped my way along the wall to the light-switch. I put my hand exactly on the place where I knew the switch to be. Instead of a switch, I touched something knuckly and hairy.

A human hand.

After a moment of terror my mind disengaged from my body, the hand, the switch and the dark room. They became distant and unreal. When another hand grabbed me by the back of my head, I screamed 'Don't'.

'Why not?' asked the murderer in a low voice.

The light snapped on.

'What the hell are you doing here?' Barnaba choked. A bread knife shook in his hand.

I have always wanted to know what it would feel like to faint for real in the presence of a man who would catch me round the waist at the last moment. The desire was as fanciful as it was futile because I was far too tough. But when I looked at Barnaba's stupefied face and the knife in his hand, I fainted without any difficulty.

And thus began the romantic part of the encounter.

Barnaba was one of my colleagues at the Psychotechnic Bureau. The staff consisted of two men, who were the bosses, and two women, Helena and myself, who were the workers. Feliks, the director, was well-built, sun-tanned and elegant and moved like a panther. He would stalk us noiselessly and pounce on us while we were brewing coffee or typing or correcting letters for him. I think he was the kind of man who could only face women from the back. Barnaba, the second boss, was slowly sagging under the weight of his head and the ideas that filled it.

Helena told me in confidence that when he was sixteen and pure and beautiful as St Dominic Savio he blew up the monument to Polish–Russian friendship in Katowice. Blew it to smithereens he did, she said with relish in her faint German accent. They gave him five years in the roughest prison in the country. She didn't recall where it was. Once free, he studied psychology, wrote his doctorate on a safe subject and got a job as a lecturer at Warsaw University. You can't keep a good man down, right? But then at his lectures he started illustrating certain sexual and mental aberrations with jokes about policemen. That did it. He was kicked out of the university and exiled to the Central Railway Station in Opole. It shows you, doesn't it? We are the gulag of the universities.

Helena couldn't be more than twenty-four and yet there was something prematurely old and cynical about her eyes and smile. She talked, smoked and gesticulated with the flair and worldly wisdom of a half-senile Oxford don being interviewed by the BBC.

After this I looked at Barnaba with a mixture of awe and curiosity. He was detached from the rest of us, a graduate of a harder university than anybody around him.

When I came to my senses he was hanging over me with a little green bottle. The room reeked of mint.

'Praise be the Lord! I thought you would never wake up. What about some coffee?'

The shock of our encounter and the conviction with which I fainted had a greater effect on Barnaba than on me. His hands were shaking as he put some mint drops on a teaspoon of sugar to steady himself. Mint drops were good for everything from stomach cramps and gallstones to nerves and chimeras. He was so distressed that I got up and made the coffee myself.

'Do you think I could have a loan of one of the sofas? I have nowhere to go.'

'Woman,' he said in a weary voice, 'do what you want but keep me out of it.'

'Do you also – I mean, do you live here yourself?'

'As you see.'

Barnaba was not in a mood for conversation. Everything about him seemed worn and tired, as if abraded to the bone by pumice stone. Only his huge eyes under their long feminine lashes kept alive the image of Dominic Savio, patron saint of boys in their struggle against self-abuse.

The true spell of Barnaba lay in his voice. It issued from a lake of caramel coated with chocolate and charcoal. It was low and dark with a slightly burnt taste and his fatigue gave gravity to the cadence.

A train rumbled into a siding near the Psychotechnic Bureau, flooding the room with crimson and green. The model tracks, semaphors, signal lights and hydrants around us took on the appearance of an underwater terminal where time was no more.

'Look,' I said. 'We are a station in Atlantis.'

We were not in Atlantis. Time was not abolished. We were in Poland and it was a historical night. Crimson, green and opal Catherine wheels were rotating in the air over Stare Miasto in Warsaw. Braids of silver swooped across Nowy Świat. A decade of senility came to a close, a decade of prodigality was about to begin.

A man who loved coalminers, spoke French and promised a little Fiat for everybody had taken over from the mastodons.

Long live Comrade Gierek!

Now was the advent of true socialism, this time for real, definitively and irrevocably, the straightening out of what had been distorted, the purifying of what had been polluted. Power to the people, bacon for the masses, joy and pleasure for everybody.

Gierek.

I register none of this. I'm turning on my cold sofa in the Psychotechnic Bureau at Opole Railway Station. I'm back to 1942, when I'm not even born.

It is snowing. I am pushing a washing machine along a forest road. Inside is my father. I am hiding him from the Germans. When I reach the railway station a Wehrmacht officer comes up to me and says: Oh, the vashing machine! How praktisch! Why don't you vash my trouses? He takes off his trousers and empties the pockets. His penis points at me like a pistol between the halves of his shirt. I'm struck to the ground. He smiles slyly and very very slowly lifts the lid.

A little reptilian head sways out of the machine, followed by the immense trunk of a dinosaur, webbed feet trashing the air.

Centuries later in another country I will see the same head in an American film. And I will cry when it pleads: Phone home! Phone home!

It snowed the next day. The whiteness all around teased us with its fraudulent innocence, as did the new page in our history. Feliks arrived in his best maroon suit with a bottle of brandy.

'Ladies and gentlemen, to the New Order!'

'Is it communism we have at last or is it going to get worse?' asked Helena.

Feliks clicked his tongue in disapproval.

'Do you know where you are sitting, my dear?'

'At the Central bloody Railway Station, where else?'

'You have no imagination. You are now in Western Europe! Rolex. Dollars. Coffee. Oranges. Chanel No. 5. Put your sweet lips a little closer to the phone.'

It was like Christmas. At two o'clock all of us except Barnaba were drunk on brandy and decadent visions. We toasted Ferguson Tractors, General Motors, Yves Saint Laurent, Paul McCartney, Johnson and Johnson, Brigitte Bardot and General de Gaulle.

Two frozen conductors/drivers/rejects who hadn't heard about the change in government quickly drank the brandies we offered them and went home. They looked like two scared rabbits who had chewed the same head of cabbage all their miserable lives. They would chew the same cabbage no matter what government was in power.

I was thinking of Barnaba. Why didn't he join us and the better future? What was he doing in his ramshackle office? I was reduced by his absence, hushed by his silence and his refusal to give of himself. I longed for the dusk to fall and the door of his office to open.

But it didn't. He disappeared for the whole evening without a word of explanation. I looked out of the windows for him a dozen times and felt foolish at my vigil. I wanted to greet him with a cup of tea and I drank my way through three pots. He came in just before dawn, his footsteps sober and confident.

Oh Barnaba, Barnaba, what are you doing to me? I thought amorously and fell asleep.

After an absurd week of celebrating the change of regime and waiting for Barnaba every night I was like a signal light stuck on red. However hard I tried to change the colour of my mind it remained fixed on my passion for Barnaba. On Sunday, when he disappeared as usual, I climbed up a ladder left behind by a window cleaner six months previously to smoke and think about my lust.

Maybe there isn't any such thing in women? Perhaps I call it lust because everybody does? But maybe it's just curiosity and the desire to be wanted? Maybe nineteenth-century medics were right when they said woman's desire was the desire of the woman for the man's desire?

'You're setting fire to yourself,' said Barnaba, suddenly entering the office below me. 'Have you seen a blue folder? I was halfway to – '

'Come on, now, you were halfway to where?'

'To church,' he said curtly in a voice that neither expected nor desired belief.

I descended from my cloud of smoke and faced him.

'I'm sorry to be so blunt. I understand that you have your private life and I don't want to interfere. But I made you fourteen cups of tea this week just to have a chat with you and every time you just evaporated.'

'What is this chat to be about?' he interrupted.

'I wanted to hear your opinion about what's going on.'

I blushed because I knew that he knew I was lying.

'What's going on where?'

'In our beloved country.'

'So you want my opinion? I'll tell you something. I have no opinions. Opinions are for careerists. I have beliefs. And they are my private business. You can quote me.'

He was aggressive and unpleasant. I had a sense that he wasn't talking to me but to some stereotype in the back of his head. The hole that a week's waiting had drilled in me filled up with anger.

'Why should I quote you or anybody else for that matter? I have my own views.'

And I went to my office slamming the door.

A moment later I heard the gentle knocking on the door which I had expected and desired.

'Look, I didn't mean to offend you. I don't know how to put it,' he sighed and put it.

'You see . . . for years in this country we've been having the same bloody identical results . . . brought about by different causes. And that is what . . . '

I shrugged my shoulders.

'Whatever.'

Helena laughed when I told her about my conversation with Barnaba.

'What a simpleton you are, Faustyna. Barnaba thinks that we are all agents sent here to watch him.'

'Nonsense.'

'There's no way you can prove that you're not. The better proof you offer the better agent you'll seem.'

'He's sick.'

'Naturally. All psychologists are.'

I was determined to prove to Barnaba that I wasn't an agent. I made deprecating remarks about the government in his presence but I could see that his watchfulness only increased. I spread the *Catholic Weekly* ostentatiously on my desk but he only asked: 'Have you suddenly become pious or something?' I told him I had a spare ticket for a political cabaret but he only took off his glasses, wiped them carefully with his sweater, looked at me with big tired eyes and said: 'Who gave you the tickets? It's impossible for ordinary mortals to get these tickets.'

While I searched for the signs of a lover in him, he searched for the signs of an informer in me.

Why did he put on a new tie?

Wasn't his voice softer than usual?

Was there a deeper meaning to his joke about the hen and the vultures?

Hadn't I seen sadness in his eyes when I mentioned that I was going to find a new place?

All these competed with

Why doesn't she go home for Christmas?

Why doesn't she try to find herself a proper place?

Why is she always awake when I come home late at night?

◊

It was our paranoias that had a romance, not we.

Until one evening he stood under my ladder with a typescript in his hand.

'Why are you always perched up there?' he asked abruptly without any preliminaries.

'You know why,' I replied, blowing smoke circles. 'I like to keep an eye on everybody.'

He ignored the provocation.

'I hear you're a good stylist. Would you check something for me?'

'Fine,' I said. 'Pass it up to me.'

So he had to climb the ladder to reach me.

It was a summary of his research on emotional disengagement in tram drivers in accident situations. I worked through it quickly, suggesting that he re-edit a few paragraphs and change a few sentences, and sent the manuscript sailing down to him page by page.

Wasn't Barnaba trying to catch the pages and look up Faustyna's skirt at the same time? And wasn't she too much of what Barnaba needed just then not to be sent there on a special mission?

'By the way, why didn't you find yourself a job in Kraków? Isn't it miserable for you here?'

'Not as miserable as it might be with my mother around.'

'Aha. There you are again. A naughty girl escaping from her terrible mummy.'

'That's none of your business,' I replied in his style. He seemed reassured.

And thus, whether he desired her or not and whether she spied on him or not the ice was broken.

Adventure Six

In which Faustyna Loses a Subversive Manuscript and Two Lovers

My initiation into Barnaba's clan took place the very next day. I expected as much. Behind the barbed wire and watchtowers of his paranoia lurked a dedicated school-boy. At another time and in another place he would have been collecting moths and butterflies. He was either one hundred per cent for you or against you. Sometime in the course of the previous evening I had crossed over the magic line that separated his tribe from a hostile world.

After work he stood in my doorway and looked around as if to check whether anybody was listening.

'There's a rally tonight. We're meeting at eight o'clock.'

'Right,' I answered obediently.

He nodded and turned on his heels. Then, turning back, 'Remember. Bring a change of clothes and a toothbrush and your identity card.'

I was worried. My only spare pair of tights was still drying on the radiator. They would never be ready for the long days and nights in the dungeons into which we were about to be cast. I turned them over like pancakes for the next two hours.

Punctually at 7.30 Barnaba stood in the doorway with a sack on his back and we marched together like Rosa Luxemburg and Karl Liebknecht to the bus-stop.

'We shouldn't be seen together. You go in the front, I go in the back. When we get off at Town Square I go clockwise in one direction, you take the other.'

'How do we meet?' I asked.

'We meet at the meeting, where else?'

When we got off the bus at Town Square nothing seemed to be going on. The pavements were silent and empty. The town was settling itself into another night of slow decay.

After twenty minutes of tramping clockwise and anti-clockwise round the square we gave up the search for the rally and went to a bar for Russian *pirogis*.

That was my introduction to the underground movement. I wasn't very impressed but I was ready for anything with Barnaba. Even if he was an anti-socialist element, a CIA agent, an imperialist, an SS man, a diversionist, a Quisling, a drug addict, a pederast, a sodomist, a leper, a Zionist and a member of the forest gangs.

I was ready but Barnaba wasn't. Seven months passed, another year ended and nothing happened. My bohemian salon in the Opole Railway Station never took off. There were no distinguished men of letters sleeping overnight on the spare chaise-longue and I never had to fight off one of the Better Young Poets. Barnaba seemed unable to get over his failure to impress me on our first dissident expedition together and he kept a polite distance. I was a fallow field, ploughed but unseeded, spending my days checking male reflexes and the long evenings reading and plotting what to do about Barnaba.

At times the phantom of my father took possession of my soul and my sofa. My father haunted every sofa, ottoman and settee wherever I stayed. He had never needed any other furniture. He slept, smoked, worked and played on a sofa.

A sofa was all he needed. It was his cosmos. When he died he left thirty-two notebooks filled with mathematical equations. One day my mother sat down with her scissors and cut the pages into neat squares. Meticulously she threaded them through a piece of string and hung them in the toilet.

I decided that the only way for me to avoid my father's fate and the magnetism of sofas was to be madly in love.

I developed the art of speculative seduction. How to waylay Barnaba? How to drag Polyphemus from his gloomy cave?

Softly softly catchee monkey.

So when he sent me another manuscript for revision I scribbled in red ink on the bottom: This is exploitation. I expect at least a bottle of cognac.

Later that evening when I was plaiting my hair and cursing Barnaba for his insensitivity, a soft tom-cat's tap teased the door. How predictable! I was disappointed that he had succumbed so easily.

But I was wrong. It wasn't Barnaba. It was Damian who stood in the doorway.

He held a small bunch of violets in his hand that he must have bought from the flower-seller in front of the station.

'Heavens! Hold on a minute.'

So – Damian instead of Barnaba. This I hadn't included in my plan. He stood more foolish and more handsome than ever in a green battledress.

'How in the name of God did you get here?'

'We're on our way to Szczecin for manoeuvres and I thought . . . '

'So you're in the army now? Well I never! Hold on a second – '

'Am I disturbing you?'

'Oh, no. Would you like some tea?'

'I'd like a cup of tea.'

His voice was clear and distinct as a bell.

A strange transfer of dispositions occurred. All my heedlessness and cheek and self-assurance passed over to him and all his shyness and confusion inundated me. Perhaps it was because I was wearing my long white nightshift for Barnaba. Little blue ducks paraded along the hem.

The situation is irreversible when a man meets a woman in a nightdress. It can lead only to one thing or, if one is lucky, to three things.

I couldn't place the lid on the kettle.

'You see, my hands are shaking,' I said to dispel the charge of joy and fear building up inside me.

He rose and approached me very deliberately, took the kettle from me, put it on the floor, took my hands in his and covered them with kisses.

And I, like the Damian of three years ago, felt like dropping everything and running.

Worse, I didn't feel any desire for him any more. The young god whose every glance had once turned my brain to pulp fiction was now a slightly inebriated lieutenant struggling to remove a pair of grey long johns. Was it that I had lived with his absence so long that I couldn't endure his presence? Or was it that I was in love with Barnaba, fixated on Barnaba all the more now that he hadn't come?

What a fool I was to wait for him like a hen of a wife! How dare he treat me so casually!

Damian's kisses became more and more insistent, more and more greedy. He was wallowing in me, hot and boyish, not like that pup Barnaba with his noble dissidence and detachment. And really, how much more beautiful Damian was. How much more giving. How stupid of me to save myself for somebody who preferred his own demons to me.

◊

And so I succumbed to Damian in a truculent embrace. How I wanted Barnaba to come in just then to punish him for his indifference!

It was only when I heard the horrible words, I love you, whispered in my ear that I sobered up.

'Please, stop. You don't know what you're saying.'

But Damian was unstoppable. He rampaged all over me with the pent-up passion of three years in the paratroopers.

'Shh, shhh, calm down,' I begged and wriggled.

Finally I managed to free myself from his embrace and put on my coat.

I sat by the window and lit a cigarette. It was the kind of scene I've always hated. The kind you get in lousy French films and paintings. Frowsy girl and sullen, post-coital boy. At such moments I could see the need for love to soften the brutality of physical desire, the need for some fluent medium to ease the transition from fucking to having a friendly cup of tea.

I tried it.

'Would you like a cup of tea?'

'Do you want me to go?' he whispered.

He too was appalled by the nakedness of our loveless bodies.

'Yes. Please go.'

I stood by the window watching the empty rails sizzle under the rain while he snapped on his battledress. It seemed to have more clasps and buttons than my great-grandmother's underwear.

He stood in the doorway, shy and stammering once more, and spoke to my left shoulder.

'Will I see you again?'

I shrank under the blue flare of his gaze. I hated myself for letting him go. I knew I would regret it. What if Barnaba never came?

'I'm sorry to be so stupid. It's the wrong day . . . '

He nodded his head.

There was a dreary finality in the thump of his heavy boots descending the stairs.

What is more lonely than a woman putting on her nightdress in an empty room when her lover has gone?

Or arranging his flowers in a jam jar?

Or making a solitary cup of coffee?

Such hennish, pointless business.

I didn't remake the bed – on purpose.

I was staring into my cup when I heard another soft tomcat at the door.

Hosanna.

Barnaba stalked in with a bottle of wine in one hand and a small bunch of violets in the other. His eyes, as indeed they ought to, fell on my nightdress, the tumbled bed and the flowers.

'Am I disturbing you?'

I could see that he was making the right connections. A long-awaited, unadulterated cloud of jealousy and desire darkened his face.

'Perhaps I should go?'

I resisted making an answer. My silence, mysterious and painful, was more effective than words.

'I'm sorry to be so late.'

I took his bottle of wine and fetched the glasses.

The situation is irreversible when a man drinks a bottle of wine with a woman in her nightdress. It can lead only to one thing, or, if one is lucky, to three things.

Barnaba, who knew as much, sat down, took off his glasses and zealously began to polish the lenses with the end of his sweater. Big eyes, long lashes, aquamarine glances at my neck and shoulders.

'I'm working on a paper for a conference in Poznań. Do you think you could have a look at it?' he asked impudently.

'For God's sake, Barnaba. Don't tell me that whatever they did to you in all those prisons of yours has turned you into a monster. Can't you forget about your papers and your bloody beliefs for half an hour?'

He lowered his eyes and stared at the blue ducks.

'Sorry to be such a disappointment,' he said, reaching into the viscous deeps of his caramel and burnt ochre voice.

'You have beautiful ankles.'

'Bees' knees and spiders' ankles,' I said for the sake of frivolity. The atmosphere was getting too lyrical for my taste.

I leaned out of the window to watch the long steel

dragons slowly creeping to their place of rest. As I expected, he put his arm around me and asked me 'Are you not cold like that?'

'Like what?'

'Why are you so cynical, woman? Why must you burst the balloon every time?' he said in his dusky voice.

What could I do but agree and cuddle up to him?

Soon the blue ducks bobbed contentedly round my neck as we all drifted out into a warm dark sea on a pullman sofa.

For a little while Barnaba's obsession with politics was deflected by, no, not by me. By an international conference on psychology. His paper was entitled 'On the Materialist View of Man and the Genesis of Psychic Disorders'. Two days before the conference he flung the manuscript on my desk and crowed, 'Faustyna, this is it. When they hear it they'll piss in their pants.'

There was triumph and vanity in his voice.

'Be careful. It's my only copy.'

I couldn't read it on the spot. I had to hitch a lift to Brzeg where I had a second job as an advisor to parents of difficult children. The job suited me down to the ground since nobody ever came to be advised and I had the three hours to myself.

The paper was brilliant. I had never read such stuff before, neither in the standard textbooks nor in the journals. The references were all to English and American books and there was no single obligatory quotation on the subject from national or fraternal sources. I was so deep in Barnaba's paper that I didn't even bother to hold out my hand for a lift. Next thing a lorry squealed to a stop beside me.

'Are you going where I'm going?' the driver smiled from the cab.

In the twenty minutes it took us to get to Brzeg he told me all about his children, his rabbits and his wife. They were all healthy and normal, thank God, and they had no need of a psychologist. From his point of view a priest was much more useful.

It was only when I settled into my office in the Health Centre that I realized I had left Barnaba's paper on the seat of the lorry.

I stumbled back to the highway like a murderer returning to the scene of the crime and hoping to revive the corpse by magic. There were thousands of lorries thundering by on the way to Kraków, Vienna, Prague. I stood nauseous with despair letting them pass, the drivers waving, smiling or making obscene gestures with their fingers. I couldn't even remember what my lorry looked like. I just stood there and stood there and stood there until it came.

'Well, I'll be damned,' the driver laughed. 'I have your papers, miss. Are you still going where I'm going?'

Never before had I felt such happiness. I was bursting with

joy. All the way home in the lorry and then on the bus I was thinking of nothing but how lucky I was and how powerful was my imagination.

It was only when I stood at the door of the Psychotechnic Bureau that my heart stopped.

I had left the manuscript on the bus.

'You left it on the lorry. And then, that very lorry happened to pass by when you were hitch-hiking back?'

Barnaba laughed a bitter wormwood laugh. 'How very convenient! And then, you say, you left it on the bus? Fantastic! A truly magical story!'

He was pacing back and forth and I could see the grey tide of paranoia rising up in him until he was engulfed in it. He sprang to the phone.

'What are you doing?'

'Woman, you're so ingenious I can't deal with you on my own. I need some assistance.'

The menace in his voice made ice crystals form in my brain.

'Edek, I've got a job for you.'

'You're not calling that bastard.'

Edek was a thuggish sociologist who always boasted that he worked for the secret police. I was sure that a guy who boasted like that couldn't really work for the police.

Whether he did or not he and Barnaba did everything they thought police interrogators should do. They tied me to a chair and shone the table lamp in my eyes.

'Now be a good girl,' hissed Edek. 'Once again the whole story from the very beginning to the very end.'

He had his hand on my knee.

'Barnaba, tell this pig to piss off!'

'First the story. What did you do with my file?'

They cross-examined me, yelled at me and blinded me with the light. What was the number of the lorry? What colour? What was the driver's name? What did he look like? Where and when precisely did it all happen? Why did I invent the story of the lorry in the first place? Who did I pass the file on to?

At first I tried to remember things. When that didn't work I tried to make a joke of it. When that didn't work I burst out crying. They threatened that if I didn't tell the truth they would dump me in some hole and nobody would hear about me ever again.

'OK, dump me,' I said through my tears with the kind of despair that would convince even KGB butchers. 'I can't tell you things that didn't happen.'

'A tough old bird,' said Edek. 'She's been well briefed. Let's start again.'

'No,' said Barnaba. 'Let her be.'

Edek looked at me disappointed.

'Let her go,' Barnaba repeated, 'and fuck off.'

Edek was like a dog that had found a strong scent. He had to be kicked away.

I was crying like a badger. The room swarmed with amoebas, red as arterial blood, that burgeoned and burst asunder wherever I looked. I groped my way back to my office and got out my suitcase. Clothes, books, candle-sticks. That was the lot.

In the bus station on Lenin Street I put up a notice: 'Important manuscript left on the bus. Please return to the Psychotechnic Bureau at Opole Central Station a.s.a.p.'

I bought myself two doughnuts and found a bench away from the drunkards where I spent the night.

Next morning I went to work to examine twenty railway-men who wanted to be engine drivers. I had to test all twenty myself since the others were not in the mood for work. Everybody was talking about the head of the psy-chology department at Wroclaw University who had no lines on the palms of his hands. He had an ape's hands. How could a man with practically no lines on his palms have made it so far?

I finished the tests as quickly as I could and I joined in the gossip. We were just having coffee when a bus con-ductor arrived with the lost folder. Barnaba rushed to him, quickly went through the pages and stuck fifty zloty in his breast pocket.

He was on his way back to his office when I stopped him.

'No, my dear, first you're going to have coffee with us.'

I knew he vaguely suspected something but he was too confused and too excited to resist.

When he held out his mug I did exactly what Laurel did to Hardy or Hardy to Laurel, I forget which. I poured the scalding coffee on his hand, then on his belly and finally on the flies of his trousers. And just as in a Laurel and Hardy film, he sat there patiently with his mug held out and looked at me with stunned eyes.

'Jesus Christ, you're some bitch,' said Helena with admiration.

Next day Barnaba, with his hand in a bandage and his balls on fire, delivered his mould-breaking lecture on the discrepancy between the socialist view of man and psychiatric practice.

To his chagrin he was not arrested for spreading anti-socialist propaganda.

Admittedly his arrest would have solved certain difficulties between us. As it was, he chose to resign from the Psychotechnic Bureau right after the conference. I wasn't to see him until ten years later, when he appeared on BBC Television as a hero of Solidarity. He had grey hair, he spoke softly and his alabaster face had the wise and well-washed expression of a Lazarus come back from the dead.

Lazaruses were two a penny in 1981.

Intermission Two

In which there are Further Signs in Heaven and Mobilization on Earth

There have been many false alarms in the tedious chronicles of our land, but one, at least, looked as if it might be for real.

On an autumnal day, the coldest of the Cold War, the hands of the nuclear clock in New York were advanced to ten minutes to midnight.

Not that anybody in Kraków gave a cobbler's fart.

For how could you worry about the Great Catastrophe if catastrophe had already occurred? How could you dread the hour of nothing-remains-after-us when everybody knew already that nothing remained except junk and the jeers of future generations? How could you dread the corpses if you were already a corpse? The whole nation was a corpse encased in a jar and left to ferment like a Borneoese carcass on its passage to higher realms.

To overcome the post-mortem indifference of our people and to help us join the civilized world, our government decided to prepare us for a nuclear attack. Old newspapers were to play a key role in this exercise. When the sirens sounded their apocalyptic wail we were to cover our heads with old newspapers, fall flat on the ground and crawl in the direction indicated by group leaders.

Two weeks before Christmas, when the sirens' alarm resounded in every nook and cranny, our nation, with the exception of antisocial elements and capitalist roaders, covered its head with *Pravda* and the *People's Tribune* and began to crawl without much conviction.

To the chagrin of the Nuclear Committees not everybody wanted to survive. Krakovians especially refused to abandon their chronic doubts as to the existence of things up to and including atom bombs. There were streets in the city, as desolate and deserted as the streets of Laredo, where lone men with their hands in the air walked tall and grateful into the blast. At the Jagiellonian University the assembled students of the Department of Modern Languages, aroused by the sight of the opposite sex sprawled on the floor, abandoned themselves to the four-part singing of Christmas carols. Football fans deserted the crawling batallions halfway to read the sports pages of the *People's Tribune*. Housewives in general ignored the high levels of radiation and walked vertically to church. They were determined not to crawl unless the priest said so.

A commendable exception to the organized chaos elsewhere were the employees of the lard factory at Poznań. They demonstrated the exemplary discipline they had imbibed with their mothers' milk and the efficiency which had been so much part of their Prussian heritage. They formed themselves into faultless crawling divisions and followed their group leaders to a man. After an exhausting passage through pools of frozen water and piles of dirty snow they were ordered to a halt. When they removed the newspapers from their heads they discovered they were at the municipal cemetery.

Right in front of them were forty mass graves freshly dug by the Nuclear Committee in anticipation of their safe arrival.

Adventure Seven

In which Faustyna Discovers Two Kinds of Scream

It will begin with a kick. A sharp, determined kick in the upper abdomen. You've had many kicks before but this one is different.

Then another kick, this time more insistent. You lift up your nightdress. There's nothing there. No bruise, no cancerous lump. Just a friendly old belly with pink fluff in the navel. You draw a deep breath to see if it will happen again. It doesn't.

You go and make yourself a cup of tea and listen to the BBC World Service. There's a war in Cambodia. The Governor of Bermuda has been assassinated along with his pet dog, a Great Dane. Pope Paul VI has written to President Idi Amin, warmly recommending missionaries to his benevolence.

All's right with the world.

And just as the Russians are about to launch another sputnik you get another kick. You run to the bathroom and look in the mirror. Your morning face is the same as usual. Maybe more drawn. It must be this silly crawling, you think. You shouldn't even have tried.

On the stairs, lifting your heavy bag you have to stop and sit down. There's a flurry of jabs that drains all your strength. You're terrified. Maybe you're going to die? And then they'll discover the mess you live in, old socks and newspapers everywhere. Not to mention other horrendous things.

The kicking stops but you know now for sure that there's something wrong.

There's somebody inside you.

The doctor looked at me quizzically.

'So what do you think is the matter with you, miss?'

'I think I'm slightly pregnant.'

He guffawed.

'Slightly? My dear you're in the fifth month at least.'

And then the usual shaming questions and shameful answers and the awful truth that I could be so absentminded.

'You're a strange case. You really hadn't noticed anything until now?'

I said nothing.

'Well, it happens. Women with irregularities get confused. But five months? You'd better decide on a father.'

The doctor's advice was reasonable but how to follow it? I was in a quandary. Was it Barnaba or Damian? Or could it be the two together? Whichever was the father, it was equally hopeless. Barnaba had disappeared God knows where and Damian had gone to Kenya to build an electric power station.

I spent whole afternoons counting, drawing diagrams, adding and subtracting, but it was no use. I'd simply have to wait and see.

I wanted it to be Damian.

No. Barnaba.

Well, perhaps Damian.

To be frank, after two years of watching tumours blossom on X-rays I was relieved to find that I was only pregnant. As long as the tumult in my belly was a sign of life and not death I could put up with it and get on with my work. Carrying somebody else inside was a complication, but then – what did I have a womb for?

Nature supported me. Everything fell into place. We were living through the first seven fat years in our history thanks to the Western banks which financed a prodigal communism to the limit. I got a scholarship from the Jagiellonian to continue my research on memory and amnesia. I found a one-room apartment in Kazimnierz in St Sebastyan Street, not far from the city centre but sufficiently far to be a deterrent to my mother.

I was happy there. I developed a set of habits which for me became synonymous with the good life ever after. I lay in bed in the mornings listening to Radio Free Europe and the BBC and re-reading yesterday's newspapers. I lost my sense of guilt about idling in bed or on a sofa. The sofa was no longer a cursed site of ancestral reverie. It was my nest in which I hatched ideas and the future generation. If one failed, I thought, the other might still succeed.

Around noon, before I went to the library, I had a cappucino in Michalik's Cave. In the evenings I dropped into the Journalists' Club for dinner and politics. I was free from the desire for intimacy with men and from most of the plagues that afflict pregnant women. Only when I bumped into things with my belly did it occur to me that I was actually in a blessed condition. Otherwise I lived a fine bachelor's life.

It must have been Nature's way of making up to me for the horrors to come.

Gradually it dawned on me that I needed bigger everything. A bigger apartment, bigger meals, bigger dresses. My person was getting beyond my means. I couldn't do anything about the apartment or the dinners in the Journalists' Club but I did have a sewing machine in my mother's place back in Prokocim.

So I started going home at weekends to assemble a majestic pregnancy dress.

My belly stuck out a mile but my mother refused to notice anything. Sometimes she would look at me strangely and ask 'Why are you making such a big dress? Are you pregnant or something?'

My secret only came out when Aunt Alina, my mother's most detested close friend, came for tea. When she saw me her first words were 'Jesus, Mary, Joseph and St Anthony, there's more in your belly, girl, than ever went in through your mouth.'

'Yes. And my mother refuses to notice. I just don't know how to tell her.'

Alina was delighted. She was dying to infuriate my mother.

When they were eating apple tart she suddenly stopped and said: 'Before I forget, Faustyna has just confessed to me that she's pregnant. She needs all your help now. Isn't that right, Faustyna dear?'

She looked her most pious and understanding while my mother fell into a tantrum.

She jumped out of her chair.

'Why didn't she tell me, her own mother?'

She raised her hands to heaven.

'Why is she saying it to strangers?'

She covered her face.

'Such shame!'

She collapsed back into the chair.

'Faustyna, why didn't you tell me?'

'I thought I didn't need to. Everybody can see.'

'You can't do this to me. You can't.'

'I don't see how not.'

'You must go to a doctor immediately and have it out or something.'

'I can't do that. It's too late.'

'You were supposed to finish your doctorate. Instead you bring me a baby. Everything is in ruins.'

'Not at all. It could be worse,' said Aunt Alina with conviction and I nodded my head eagerly.

'What do you mean worse? I can't imagine anything worse. She brings me . . . And who is the father, if I may ask?' she said, with the old familiar hysteria rising in her voice.

'And what does he do?' added Alina, expecting to hear something wonderful.

'It has two fathers.'

As usual when my mother was determined to be angry I was determined to goad her further into a rage. But oddly enough the idea of two fathers flummoxed the two of them completely.

Aunt Alina was the first to recover. She had gone over to the other side.

'My dear,' she said bitterly. 'I don't think you're taking it all seriously enough. It is another life after all.'

'Yes, I understand. But I haven't chosen it. It has chosen me.'

'What?'

'As a bearer, I mean.'

Aunt Alina looked at me with eyes big as teacups.

As always on such occasions, my mother's voice acquired a whining pitch and a Belorussian accent.

'I told you, I told you. She'll deny all responsibility. I don't know where she's getting these ideas from. I won't survive it. I want to die.'

'Just a moment,' said Aunt Alina. 'What do you mean it has chosen you?'

I could see by the medical expression on her face that she thought I was going cuckoo.

I knew exactly what I meant. The air was full of souls clamouring to be born. One had been quicker than the others and took advantage of my situation. It wasn't a part of me in any possessive sense. It was a totally different person who chose me to release her into the world.

I didn't explain my natal theory to my mother and Aunt Alina. I got back to sewing my dress while the two of them sat at the table, ate their cakes and lamented my stupidity.

After midnight my mother's bedroom door opened.

'It won't happen under my roof. I'm too old for a scandal. Go back to Kazimierz and don't let me see you ever again.'

In the morning when I was packing she was terrified in case her harsh words would drive me to suicide. She gave me 200 zloty and said 'Don't do anything foolish now.'

But when I sat down and calmly drank my coffee and ate all the ham in the fridge and read my newspaper as if nothing had happened, she fell into a rage once again.

'Faustyna, I can't imagine you having this baby. You're not able to look after yourself much less a child. Something terrible is going to happen. I can see it. You're going to damage this baby. Surely you're going to damage it.'

What she really meant was that I was like my father. I spent most of my life on a sofa reading books and newspapers. Away from the sofa I was incompetent and a danger to myself and others.

My mother in her hunger for distress did what she had

always done. Instead of encouraging me she pondered my weaknesses and brooded over my resemblance to my father. She had harassed him to death with her love and worry. I decided she wasn't going to do the same to me or whoever was inside me. An invisible shield protected us from her terror.

I spent the 200 zloty on tidbits. I wanted to assure the child that it was coming into a good world, a world where there were bars of halva, pink slices of *poledwica*, plums coated in chocolate, spicy game sausages and poppy-seed cakes.

It was only when I saw other pregnant women being fussed over by their husbands that I felt dejected. I would have loved to send Damian or Barnaba out for strawberry ice-cream in the middle of the night or to have one of them vacuum-clean for me and the other lever me into bed when I became big as a barrel.

In the ninth month of pregnancy I had a revelation. One morning, when I spread the *Voice of Kraków* on the ironing-board I used as a desk, I realized I didn't give a hoot about psychology. There was a new hunger in me.

Some pregnant women become avid for the taste of coal or sauerkraut. I hankered for the acrid taste of political intrigue. Politics was what I wanted. Large dollops of it. Psychology was as colourless and odourless as a Canadian. All around me were gamy cuts of *realpolitik*. They grew ripe in the air, the city was tangy with them. It was the time of posters, anniversaries, speeches and referenda. Thousands of believers were waiting for a new faith while shops sold beef marked 'merchandise of secondary freshness'.

I felt that I had dreamt all my life away. I was about to be born.

Julia was in no hurry to join me in the outside world even though I had a belly big as a globe and I could hardly carry the two of us around.

On St Andrew's night I was sitting at home reading Weber when the bell rang. When I opened the door a huge bottle of vodka dangled in front of my nose and a drunken crowd of St Andrew's merrymakers from my Institute came tumbling down the corridor. They rushed into my room and settled on chairs and tables and on the sink like cackling hens on roosts.

'Now drink up. It's to help him to come out.'

I took a little sip.

'More, more.'

Another one, then.

'Ohhhh, she's drinking.'

'Ohhhhh, something's coming out.'

'No, it isn't.'

'Give the woman more vodka.'

They watched me with buttery-eyed intensity. They demanded that this birth should happen right away, on the spot, without further delay.

But Julia wouldn't budge.

So they sat around patiently for a couple of hours, like poachers tickling a trout, and talked of the birth of monsters.

When they had all gone I began to melt.

It's Kraków 1973. It's November, so you put on a hat and a coat and you wobble to the nearest hospital. There's nobody at reception. You hear sounds of distant music and laughter. It's St Andrew's night, Glen Miller and Duke Ellington and you dripping with your cargo.

Hello, you shout, hello.

A sulky young goose appears in the corridor with 'Jesus, what a time you've chosen' written across her face.

All right, all right. Your name and health book number?

No, we can't register you without the health book.

Sorry, it's impossible to admit you without the book.

Jesus, she asks me what she should do. Go get your health book, missus.

OK OK if you can't walk you can't walk. Next time you bring your book.

You are brought to a huge room with twenty empty beds. Wait there. An hour passes. You howl with pain while you wait. A nurse with a flush of Malaga on her cheeks sticks her head round the door.

What are you screaming for? There's no reason.

I'm in terrible pain.

Everyone is in pain.

You think, this is how Sovietization works. You shouldn't express your pain. Everybody knows that you're in pain. It's superfluous to express what everybody knows.

A young doctor steaming with gin examines you briskly and goes out whistling a Glen Miller tune. You can hear the party down the corridor. You envy that room full of flat bellies and painless bottoms. You remember that walking helps to speed up the delivery so you try to get off the bed but you can't because of the searing pain.

The phone rings in the abandoned duty room.

It is Inspector Fox from the Flying Squad in Scotland Yard. You have to answer this call, your life depends on it. So you drag your body to the duty room praying that it won't stop ringing. It goes on ringing. As you crawl along the gunshot wound in your belly opens wider. You leave a slick of blood along the floor but you must go on. Just as you're about to grab the phone it stops ringing. You collapse back in sobs, hugging your gaping belly.

Then it rings again. Scotland Yard doesn't give up easily. Inspector Fox knows that you're here, knows how you are suffering as your life drains away.

You grab the phone.

Hello, I want to enquire about a patient. Mrs Faustyna Falk, has she delivered yet?

Aunt Alina's voice breaks the reverie.

No I haven't. I'm just doing it. Please don't disturb me.

◊

My voice was thick and coarse. It was almost male in its coarseness. It gave Aunt Alina a bad fright. She decided that the situation was so improbable that later she denied that she had ever talked to me during my delivery.

But then, as my great-grandmother said, I lived in the realm of lower probabilities.

You crawl back to the bed. The party is finishing and the last revellers are giggling and chasing one another in the corridors. In the tired dirty dawn an old midwife appears beside you. You grab her hand.

Jesus, if every patient pulled my hand like that I would be a cripple by now.

Please do something, you beg.

Yes, but first you do it. It can't be the other way round.

But it can. She goes to the door to greet another woman who is in the twelfth station of her Via Crucis. A nervous husband stuffs a tight roll of green banknotes in the midwife's pocket. The midwife becomes gentle and docile and, with her arm around the young woman's waist, helps the poor suffering creature to her bed. She rings for a doctor. He too becomes protective and professionally active once the husband passes him a bottle of brandy.

The young mother screams.

You scream.

There are two kinds of scream in the world. One that is backed up by dollars and one that isn't. In the Maternity Ward you discover the indifference that blunts the edge of a dollarless scream. Such screams make nothing happen and only exhaust the screamer.

I couldn't bring myself to give her a name. It was one thing to give birth to her another to impose a name that would define her prematurely and stamp her for life. I was paralysed by the power I had over her. To make her a Kathleen or a Sylvia or a Lucretia. Better for her to grow up and choose a name for herself or for some overwhelming fate to impose one on her, make her a Ruth or a Magdalena or an Isolda. For the sake of peace and to fulfil the legal requirements, I called her Marianna. But at home I called her Little Pumpkin, and left the question open.

When she grew up she called herself first Dominika and then Julia. Her boyfriend calls her Foka. My mother (who called her Wanda after her mother in the hope that the name would stick) accepted her at once but she kept on whinging to punish me for my cheek in having a child. She couldn't reconcile my absentmindedness and the little girl.

I had recurring nightmares. I would put the baby in the chest of drawers, go to a party and forget all about her. I would return after a few days, exhilarated and delighted with myself. Then I would remember Marianna. I would run to the drawers and open them in a frenzy. I opened them again and again feeling their cold insides with my hands and finding nothing.

Intermission Three

In which Nothing of Any Great Interest Happened for Six and a Half Years Except that the People's Republic Touched Rock Bottom and Nobody Noticed the Difference

Adventure Eight

In which Some People are Lucky and Some are Not and there is no Means to Discover Why

There were two large windows in my new apartment in Krzemionki. The east window looked out on a small square where a scabby weeping willow hunched under the relentless gaze of the housewives from the surrounding tenements. The west window faced on to the street and was crossed by five parallel telegraph wires.

One September evening Aleksander sat opposite the west window and composed his Pigeon Symphony Opus 3. Every evening, when the traffic eased, the pigeons perched like notes on a stave opposite our apartment and Aleksander copied them down. He hummed their positions to himself, a, h, c, e, patiently orchestrating the fidgets of the dowdy birds.

I told him his plagiarizing from nature was worse than socialist realism but he said no, not at all, he was Poland's first ecological composer.

I stood at the open east window watching a crowd of neighbours gathering under Staś and Joanna's balcony.

Staś and Joanna stood on the balcony in their pyjamas, holding hands.

Jump! somebody yelled. Jump before they get you!

You could hear the pounding of a mallet coming from their apartment.

'They're raiding Staś and Joanna again,' I shouted out to Aleksander.

But he was too engrossed with his synthesizer, playing variations on the evening's score of birds.

Joanna blessed herself and began to clamber over the rail.

Come on! We'll catch you!

It's too high for her! cried Staś and half-heartedly tried to hold her back.

It's only the second floor, for God's sake!

Joanna let go of the balcony rail and fell with a savage yell into the arms of Jozek the bricklayer, who toppled over on top of her. A leather mummy of a secret policeman loomed behind the glass door.

Jump! Jump, you idiot!

Staś looked around, took fright and flung himself down with the abandon of a schoolboy leaping from a diving board. There was a dull thud as he hit the ground. The crowd closed over him. A woman shot an accusing finger at the policemen on the balcony.

Murderers!

The neighbours rushed Staś's limp body to a little Fiat, stuffed him in, pushed wailing Joanna on top of him and drove off with a roar.

'They've escaped!' I shouted to Aleksander.

'And so have my fucking pigeons. Are we ever to get any peace and quiet in this place?'

The leather mummy threw bits and pieces of a printing press into the street. He held his booty triumphantly over his head before hurling it down with a grunt. There was an archetypal ecstasy in his posture, a memory of icons smashed in Byzantium and synagogues gutted in Berlin and Paris.

Just to be on the safe side, I hid my files in the laundry basket. The notes were for my study 'Why Solidarity and Where Does it Lead To?'

When I got back to the window, the tenement children led by Julia were dancing round the willow singing 'The Old Bear is Sleeping Like a Log.'

'I've got an idea,' said Aleksander, talking less to me and more to the genius that sat in his head. 'I'll use the bear tune to scatter the pigeons in the andante. That's just what I need. What do you think?'

If an atom bomb exploded you'd put it to use in your bloody symphony.

Julia waved up to us and made a V-sign.

Aleksander bowed and blew her a kiss.

Aleksander never ceased to confound me. He embodied one of the most puzzling riddles in the Design of Things. He was blessed. The whole Opalewski family was blessed. I met them at their annual get-together in their villa in Zakopane. They sat under crystal chandeliers like a convocation of angels and told one another risqué anecdotes about the world of men. All the Opalewskis were tall and comely and lived into their nineties. They had lots of hair and lots of teeth and one generation outbid the other in the acquisition of love, fame and fortune. Success came to them effortlessly; they knew nothing of desperation or failure, they never needed to bribe God with prayers or penny candles.

There they were around the table, famous artists, philosophers, scientists and businessmen. Joking about communism with the insolent levity of voyeurs. Whatever the system, their *baraka* would always transcend it. Aleksander wrote his Pigeon Symphony out of the same heroic indifference as his brother designed neo-gothic palaces for African dictators.

Was it on a whim that God had decided to like the Opalewskis? Equally, was it his divine caprice to turn his face against Joanna and Staś? They had done everything to merit his grace but all in vain. The fate of their families was a dreary Polish tale: sacrificial struggle in national uprisings, all the best sons hung and quartered, those who didn't die on the gallows died of cancer. Staś, once the youngest university professor in the country, had a ban placed on all his publications. Joanna, a leading lawyer, went through two miscarriages, had a heart condition and endured half a dozen plagues she said she wouldn't dare to mention. They lived on nothing in a small apartment from which they published an independent university bulletin.

There wasn't an altar or an icon in the whole of Kraków they hadn't prayed before. Yet God took every opportunity to kick them around and to extinguish their tribe.

He had sent a raven of paranoia to perch on Joanna's shoulder.

Do you see those two guys at the bus stop? it croaked when we went out shopping together. Those two guys in grey coats. They never take a bus.

Have you noticed the new plumber doing the rounds of the tenements? Not a grease stain on his overalls!

Look at the red car with Warsaw plates. It's been there for days. Let's run.

There were no innocent objects in Joanna's world. Walking with her I had the feeling that the city was like a great quiescent monster that we mustn't provoke. If we did, the whole street, telegraph poles and all, would come cantering down to the Vistula after us. There were ears and eyes everywhere, even in her shoes. I can't put them on without checking if something has been planted there, she said helplessly two days before the raid. I'm going mad.

I tried to slip into Joanna's paralysed soul; I touched a lamp, a vase, an armchair, and tried to imagine how they might betray me. But their warm candour resisted my mistrust.

'What are you up to?' asked Aleksander when he caught me feeling the shiny undersides of the rubber plant.

'Just checking its innocence.'

As always, he liked the idea without bothering to enquire what it meant.

It was Julia who persuaded me to take on Aleksander. He met all her requirements for a father. He doesn't smoke, he doesn't drink, he has a piano at home, he's famous, he smells nice, he plays with me and he kisses you on the hand when he says goodbye. Breathlessly she would re-enumerate his virtues every time she sensed an approaching end.

She spied on us. Many times I found her eavesdropping behind doors or keeping vigil outside our bedroom.

'What's wrong, Little Pumpkin?'

'I can't sleep when you don't talk. I just wanted to see if you were talking to Olek.'

We were on our last batteries, calmly observing the disintegration of our relationship like two characters out of Marguerite Duras. *He wept. She wept. There was death under their skins*. We ought to have been in Strasburg or Vienna. I should have been a tubercular teenager in a gauze dress with nothing better to do than weep, make love and play Vivaldi.

I both dreaded and desired Aleksander's departure. I had already begun to miss his insolent detachment from the here and now, his hummings and stray chords, his gigglings with Julia and his mute protests against the vulgarity of my pursuits and the mussiness of my hair.

To avoid the bristling silence of the evenings I sneaked out to the neighbours to join in the communal rite of TV watching. To clap and whistle when bright-eyed Solidarity newsreaders cheerfully reported the growing rate of infant mortality, disasters at coalmines, stifling corruption and the total ruin of our economy. We listened to bad news with the vindictive triumph of terminally ill patients who had finally got confirmation of their worst suspicions. Didn't we say so? Hadn't we known it all along?

As last we heard how hopeless it all was. How incurable. We were thrilled. The awful truth restored to us our humanity.

In this general mood of pessimistic exaltation people smiled at one another and gave flowers to strangers in the street. You hardly noticed bus strikes, so suddenly patriotic and punctilious were the owners of private cars. Nobody drank but everybody sang and said prayers. There was an orgy of kneeling down. People clustered round church doors like swarms of bees. From the baroque sky poured down the plaintive hymns of Joan Baez, the benedictions of John Paul II and the tears of the Virgin Mary with Lech Walesa in her lapel. He sat there eating a lard sandwich and looking confidently into the future. There were crosses shining in his eyes.

I went to conferences and meetings where garrulous men

with glamorous stubble agonized over decades of stupidity and blunder. Our country was short of everything except words. Rising above the fug of cigarette smoke, stale sweat and Dettol was the stench of verbiage.

If you rant for days on end in a room without doing normal things like cooking dinner or playing with a child or washing your hair, words begin to spoil. The smell is a mixture of lead, liquorice and slaked lime. Opening windows and doors doesn't get rid of it.

All over Poland there are rooms reeking with this effluvium. They should have been entombed in concrete like leaky reactors and left to detoxify for a thousand years.

When I returned from one of these rooms Aleksander would say, 'You smell of corpses.'

He seemed to look down on me from a great height and I had to crane my neck to look up at him. He was heedless of what went on in the street below the pigeon staves. He lived in his head in a place without history or suffering. He composed symphonies. He looked after his body. He cooked elaborate dinners from an Italian cookbook. He gave piggyback rides to Julia.

On Saturday afternoons when human beings saw a happy threesome strolling through Planty Park, the extra-terrestrials perched on the turrets of the Wawel Castle saw only Julia and Aleksander. I wasn't there. I was too dense and turbid to register on their astral lenses.

◊

I wondered how Aleksander would bring about what had already occurred on the subtle planes. Another woman? A scholarship to Vienna? My own good? Allergies?

He wasn't an avant-garde composer for nothing. He brought our love to an end on Julia's birthday with a clangorous cadence. He put roses on our dinner-plates and he dressed up in his concert tails to serve us *osso buco alla Romana*. Then he played Mozart records and danced awkward minuets with Julia.

We should have been in Strasburg or Vienna, where there would have been filaments to join music and laughter to a secure, festive city. We should have waltzed in a place where there were memories of waltzes and where ancestral eyes would have approved the dance.

Smetek, the devil of doubt, possessed me. He hung an interrogative at the end of every thought, of every glance, I gave Aleksander. Why such an implacable gap between silver arpeggios and broken glass on the streets? Who was this couple holding hands on the way to the bedroom? Who hesitated in the arms of her lover? Why did their caresses and words say different things? And who turned the light off just then?

— You can't go on like this. Julia needs a full-time mother.

— You can't shut us up in your ivory tower.

— You're not living in the real world.

— You're the one who's escaping.

– For the last time. Give up this political nonsense. It's leading you away from us.

– I don't ask you to give up your music. Where is it leading?

– To Vienna. I've won the competition.

– The Pigeons Opus 3?

– Yes.

Marguerite Duras again. *He wept. She wept. There was death under their skins.*

The door burst open.

'If he goes I go with him,' shouted Julia, pouting her Damian lips and frowning her Barnaba brows. 'You can stay here all by yourself.'

I wrapped a blanket round me and dragged her back to her room.

'I know, I know. I'm a very bad mother. If you leave me I'll just rot here.'

'You will. Because you don't love us. You only love books and meetings.'

'That's not true, Little Pumpkin. I need somebody to look after me.'

'Yes, but who's going to look after me?'

'Well, let's look after one another then.'

We had played out this scene many times before and we both knew our lines by heart.

Aleksander left behind in Kraków a woman who felt she was coming asunder along with the world around her.

She had a past there, a daughter here (how cold her hand was!), a mother somewhere else, a lover dismissed, two careers on the shelf. People could see through her skin as through a string shopping bag. They could see the mad jumble inside. Bits of her stuck out like groceries – a green plume of carrot tops, a pair of pig's feet, a bottle of vinegar.

It was from this hodgepodge that Feliks rescued her, as he rescued thousands of others.

Adventure Nine

In which Faustyna Discovers the Hostility of Things

I saw Feliks for the first time when he spoke to the assembled workers in the canteen of an underwear factory.

My dear ladies. For forty years we've been allowed to talk only about success. To write it, paint it, film it, sculpt it, weave it, knit it, you name it. At last, my friends, we can have a good look at the Emperor's clothes. And what do we see? Well, the closer we look the stranger it is. There's no Emperor! There's a void under the tattered rags. Not even a decent pair of knickers! Ladies, let me tell you. We created this phantom. We let it rule us for forty years. Now we must create ourselves.

He was small and mobile with a dark gypsy face and flying hands. He wasn't handsome but he had a teasing charisma that touched and troubled me. As he spoke his words became broad-shouldered and muscular. They stood six feet tall and raised an ephebic head above the crowd.

Why is it only men that can engender this power? Why doesn't a woman's voice excite the erogenous zones of a crowd? Why don't her words weave an erotic nimbus around her sufficient to make up for a dumpy figure or eyes too close together?

(Search me.)

Who is this man? I asked again and again until I pieced together a legend.

He had lived seven lives and had vanquished seven foes. He sought to be wise so he ate lots of fish and studied Spinoza. After he became wise he wanted to be rich. So he turned to trade and trade led him to the black market and the black market led him to jail. In jail he returned to Spinoza and decided to be honest. So he went to the country where honest people live and studied beekeeping. In spite of himself, as it were, he made a small fortune selling honey and dried forest mushrooms to the French and West Germans. But the authorities failed to appreciate the avant-garde nature of his pursuits and closed him down. His next incarnation was as a quality control manager in a shirt factory where the women called him the poisoned dwarf.

When the hour of freedom struck, the dwarf took command of the strike committee. Power made him tall, romantic and alluring. After two weeks of strike, he emerged shaggy and feverish from the factory to negotiate with the *voivod* and the First Secretary. He refused to accept their conditions. There were principles at stake.

The factory women fell at his feet. Take me, take me,

they cried, do with me what you want, so powerful was he and so grown in stature.

His eyes fell on Mira, who was the kind of perverse princess only a Polish shirt factory could produce. Three months before she wouldn't give him the time of day and now she opened to him all her treasures.

(Fair play to her.)

When the government of the People's Republic decided to consult the people for the first time in forty years, Feliks was invited to Warsaw to take part in the final round of talks. He took Mira and the factory car and a chauffeur and off they went to Warsaw like Lord and Lady Muck.

When I heard Feliks addressing the crowds I dropped my string-shopping-bag-self for good.

'If there's no Emperor, who shall we blame for all the mess?' I asked him in the Café Gwiazdeczka after the meeting.

'Everything in its right time,' he said. 'For the present a bunch of pious, harmless Poles looks so much more appealing on Western television than a pack of blood-thirsty hounds. Can we change the subject? Where did you get your divine head of red hair?'

'My grandfather was an Irish fiddler from Ballinasloe.'

'And mine a one-eyed Albanian acrobat from Shkodur.'

We fell for one another from the very first lie.

Our main task became: how to get rid of Mira.

'You can't get rid of Mira,' said Feliks. 'She's like an ink stain. The moment she soaks into the fabric, caustic soda won't remove her. The best we can do is to escape from her.'

We met at the market in Kleparz when Feliks was supposed to be chairing a subcommittee on the distribution of medicines in Krakowskie.

We strolled among piles of onions, potatoes and carrots and crusty barrels of sauerkraut, inhaling the vegetable odour of our infatuation and keeping an excited eye out for Mira.

Or we took a bus to Krak's Mound near the village of Mogila to lose ourselves among the beech trees when Feliks should have been addressing dairy workers on the problem of adulterated milk and Mira was fruitlessly searching for us in the cowsheds.

Or we would hire a landau and drive round the Barbican in romantic circles, aware that at every moment Mira might appear round the corner and interrupt an interview on 'Why Solidarity and Where Does it Lead To?'

Mira became an essential ingredient in our affair, a shadowy pursuer whose long silhouette on the walls behind us gave our romance a cinematic flourish. Wherever we went she was the indispensable third.

I never met her except in my dreams and in my dreams she was always a man.

Julia began to tell me bedtime stories about spiders and

webs and hapless bees. I grew afraid of her. They were parables of my secret adventures. They always ended with the bees locked up in separate cells.

'Can't you change the ending and let them live happily ever after?' I asked.

'No,' she shook her golden head and looked at me coldly with her beautiful eyes. 'Do you want *me* to tell a lie?'

I don't know why – perhaps because I felt an urge to rebel against her autocracy – but I didn't tell Julia about my affair with Feliks. I knew it tormented her and yet I didn't tell her. I would come home with a beard rash or a button missing from my blouse or a piece of heather in my hair and she would meticulously point it out to me. Finally I got angry.

'You're a seven-year-old brat and your mother has the right to her own life. I don't have to explain myself to you, do I?'

Her eyes filled with tears which she was too proud to let fall.

'OK, do what you like. But I won't tell you things any more either.'

Julia, unlike me, was consistent. She kept her word. She became secretive and patronizing to punish me for my lapses into adolescence.

Adolescence, I discovered, is not a stage in life you grow out of. It stays inside you as a permanent possibility, like the ability to swim or ride a bicycle. Even at sixty you find yourself saying the same foolish words and feeling the same devastation that you said and felt at sixteen.

In the factory yards, cafés and conference rooms taken over by Solidarity, I rediscovered my adolescence and the fatuity of the myth of growth. I took the leash off my long legs and red hair and wicked tongue. I was the girl in the ad for Furstenberg, head thrown back, regal breast and a retinue of laughing dissidents around me. They were half-baked poets, frustrated lawyers, pissed-off mathematicians, who found in Solidarity a compensation and a deliverance from their fraudulence and failure. And beside me stood my Napoleon, hardly up to my shoulder, his left hand thrust far into his jacket, his mouth blowing a speech bubble: I feel a great big tit. I shone and sparkled. I coquetted the rebels and they coquetted me.

The same adolescent brew of flirtation and power games infused the talks between Solidarity and our government. The Café Gwiazdeczka was a replica of the Belvedere where the apparatchiks dallied with the rebels and the rebels winked at the apparatchiks. The air was full of allusions and courtesies and nobody said what he meant.

My second adolescence was as brief as the first. While I was gallivanting the spiders were spinning.

It took me a while to put things together. At first I blamed my absentmindedness and the excitement of having Feliks. It started from things I said being repeated to me by people I hardly knew. I spent whole evenings trying to puzzle out how and where and when. Sometimes when I returned to the apartment before Julia got home I had a jittery sense that somebody had moved the carpet or opened the washing machine or shifted the papers on my desk. The telephone rang at odd hours but there was nobody at the other end, only a silent octopus reaching a tentacle into my bedroom. My letters began to arrive in transparent plastic bags with a note: Damaged in transit. My hands trembled when I opened them.

I lost sleep. I was afraid to fall asleep because I didn't know who I'd be or where I'd be when I woke up. I began to keep a lookout, standing for hours in the east and west windows, watching the square and the street, suspicious of everything that stood still. Every creak, every step on the stairs, brought me to the door where I listened and listened.

From the street and the staircase the terror moved indoors and took hold of my things. Even my favourite armchair threatened me and there was a potential Judas lurking in the wardrobe. To Julia's surprise I organized vast and thorough cleaning expeditions to cover my search for hidden microphones. I looked with new, strategic eyes at the balcony. It was too high to jump from and too low for suicide.

I felt for the first time the abject helplessness of living among people who could do nothing if I disappeared without a trace. In my desperation I thought that even

Julia, with her angelic looks and devilish intelligence, hardly needed me.

So that's what it feels like, that's what it means to be colonized by an alien intelligence.

'That's it. That's it exactly,' said Joanna. 'You're becoming a wreck, just like me.'

She kicked a stone into the Vistula. We watched till the last ring of the stone's plea for help had disappeared.

'What am I to do?' I asked Feliks.

'Do? Why should they possibly be after you?'

'But they are,' I kicked a stone into the Vistula.

'I don't think so. You're not that important.'

'I see.'

He thought for a moment.

'I know. They're bugging you because of me.'

His male vanity extended even to wanting a monopoly on persecution. We sat on the bench to watch the ducks in the urinous river. He went on blithely:

'There's not much you can do once they're after you. If we win it won't matter. If we don't then both you and I . . .'

He pointed with his chin towards the river.

'Don't stew in your own juice. Ring everybody, all your friends, aunts, uncles, grannies, and tell them that the slimy bastards are after you. Don't agree to any meetings.'

'What if they round me up?'

'Don't sign anything.'

'What if they lock me up?'

'Don't be a martyr. I'm pissed off with martyrs. Give me a kiss.'

So I went through my address book from A to Z and told my dread to everybody. Feliks was right. As soon as I publicized my fear it drained off into the sump of collective anxiety and I could sleep fitfully again.

The French existentialists were wrong. Inauthentic life in the face of terror and uncertainty is the only liveable one.

Like a swarm of Cassandras we spend the last months of freedom hawking divinations and predictions.

The prophets said: There will be a Russian invasion before winter.

They said: We don't need an invasion, we can do it for ourselves. There will be civil war.

They said: The Pope will see us through.

They said: Read Nostradamus. Solidarity will win and a golden age will follow. We'll get Vilnius back too.

They said: The West will come to our rescue. They have learnt from history that we are the Heart of Europe.

They said: Rubbish. We're sitting with only one buttock in Europe. We are West Asians.

Adventure Ten

In which both Faustyna and the People's Republic Endure Coitus Interruptus

We were right in the middle of doing the Bridge Over the River Kwai. It was getting harder and harder to hold on. The pillow kept slipping from under my bottom and my head was snared between the headboard and the mattress.

'Don't lose it now! Don't lose it for Christ's sake,' cried Feliks in pre-coital desperation.

He thrust at me with a frenzy half-generated by the ripe bodies in his pocket *Kama Sutra*. Like a good tactician he had worked over the ground in advance and guided me into Position 37 or 17 or whatever with tiny furtive slaps to my belly and thighs.

I was in fragments. A breast to the right, eye blazing to the left, lips in the centre, gibbous haunches raised to heaven.

(Hold on! If the pillow is under your bottom, . . . and your haunches in the air . . . I don't think you've got it quite right.)

(Consult the Kama Sutra *dear boy.)*

I was fractured and spliced like a cubist painting. I gazed at parts of my anatomy I had never seen before. The brute physicality of limbs and joints at grotesque angles numbed my desire.

There was a very bad smell coming from the kitchen. This smell was my only hope of release.

'What is it?' I asked.

'What's what?'

'That smell. It must be the rubbish. I asked you to take it out, remember?'

I was smarting inside. The Bridge Over the River Kwai buckled painfully.

'Just another thirty seconds,' Feliks begged.

'I can't go on with the stench of dead hippopotamus in the room.'

'Jesus and Mary.'

Despondently, Feliks collapsed at my side. All the jizz had gone out of him, yet he managed to maintain a bruised, purple erection.

While I unwound myself from the gyres of tantric love, Feliks punched his way into his pyjamas and spoke tender words of consolation to his penis.

It was 1.30 a.m. on the morning of December 13, 1981. It was snowing.

'Don't be too long!' I called after him to ease his pride and show him a bit of affection.

These were the last words I ever spoke to Feliks.

My last and only bohemian of the boudoir! None of my previous lovers could make me laugh and climax at the same time. Out of bed they were gay or witty or mad, but in bed, to a man, they were tragedians. Feliks was the exception. For him sex was comic. It was a circus, a carnival, a tantric riot on a temple wall. The lingam, he would say, should be chilly as an ice lolly and the gates of jade as warm and lubricious as a freshly baked doughnut dipped in syrup.

And he would go for a run in the snow and come back to try it.

(And how was it?)

(Don't be nosy.)

Or he would accompany his couplings with a running sports commentary: Wolicki, Wolicki has the ball at his feet. He's pressing towards the goalmouth now. He's nearly there. He falls! He falls! No! He's on his feet again! This boy's good. This boy's very good, There's nothing to stop him now. Fifteen metres, ten metres, five metres. Can he do it? He can! He can! The goalkeeper tenses. I can see the sweat on her brow from here! Her nipples are red and hard as rowan berries. She's tight as a bow, waiting for Wolicki's final assault! And here it comes! Here it is! A long, low, hard ball to the back of the net!

There was a rattattat outside. What was it to be this time? I sashayed to the door and opened it lasciviously. The young soldier on the landing nearly fainted with embarrassment. So I covered my lower bodily stratum as best I could with Feliks's *Kama Sutra* and my upper bodily stratum with my left arm.

'What is it?'

The soldier gave me a trembling salute.

'I . . . I'm sorry, citizen. Just checking if, ehm, a Mr Feliks Wolicki lives here.'

Automatically I said what every woman covering for her man would say.

'No. Nobody of that name lives here.'

Even as I spoke I felt a metaphysical chill at the nape of my neck. Perhaps I should have said just the opposite? What should I have said?

Before I could get my wits about me the soldier was halfway down the stairs, mumbling apologies.

With my blood standing still I switched off the lamp and went to the window. A military lorry ablaze with light had settled like a UFO in the middle of the courtyard. Two aliens in steel helmets stood on either side of Feliks. A little white skullcap of snow had settled on his head. He pointed desperately to his pyjamas, to the bucket in his hand, up to our window.

Christ, what had I done? By the time I had my pants and pullover on, the UFO with Feliks aboard had vanished.

I don't know how long I stood in the yard letting the snowflakes bruise my eyes.

You idiot, you stupid idiot! If only you hadn't been so pernickety and endured Position 43 for another few minutes! It was horrible to think of bright little Feliks with his love of high jinks in bed taken away like that, and in his pyjamas too.

Then it hit me. He had been dragged away by soldiers! Why soldiers? Does it mean . . . I raced back upstairs to the phone. It was dead. I switched on the radio. It was playing Chopin. I changed the station. It was playing Chopin. All the stations were playing Chopin.

God wasn't just resting on Sunday 13th. He was entirely comatose and had abandoned the world to its folly. Instead of the usual Sunday morning Mickey Mouse series on TV there was a death mask in dark glasses intoning a list of rules and penalties.

Violation of rule twenty-one: death penalty.

Violation of rule twenty-two: death penalty.

Violation of rule twenty-three: seven years imprisonment.

So that was it! While Feliks and I were tangling ourselves in tantric love-knots, the Poles had done something unprecedented in their long history of self-abuse: they had invaded themselves.

When I went to fetch Julia from the Janickis' there were tanks jolting and farting at street corners. Dazed young recruits with downcast eyes turned their backs on us, mortified at what they had just done. The sun sharpened its teeth on their bayonets.

There were armed males everywhere. I had never been so struck by the overwhelming maleness of violence and power, by its eagerness to sheath itself in metal and leather and brass buckles. When I trudged home hand in hand with Julia we passed groups of young men who had surrendered to compulsory virility, defeated by their heavy boots, Sam Browne belts and long bullswool coats.

They in their coarse green trousers and belts and guns and we in skirts and panties and bras – how could we be said to inhabit the same planet, much less be members of the same species?

Julia cut through my sentimental cluckings. She had been well briefed by the Janickis. She explained all the rules of martial law to me, emphasizing the time of curfew.

'From now on you'll have to be home at ten o'clock,' she said with satisfaction. 'If not you'll be shot.'

The devils sniggered under the icy pavements.

Like my father, I have never expected much from life as such. But from Sunday 13th on I expected even less. The one thing I did expect was the archetypal knock on the door.

They come when I'm washing my hair. They ransack the apartment. Julia screams Mammy! Mammy! Mammy! Pages of my manuscript litter the floor. They paste me to the wall with big words: Patriotism . . . Motherland . . . Reasons of State . . . Anti-national . . . Anti-state . . . Treason . . . Diversionist . . . Whore! They kick me. I can't see through the confusion of my wet hair and tears.

They came a few days after Christmas. A sad gentleman in a large fur coat and a soldier with an automatic pistol.

'I'm very sorry, madam, but, how to say it?, you are interned, so to speak.'

The fur coat seemed to be utterly amazed at hearing himself say this.

I wasn't surprised and yet I went soft at the knees.

'Please come in.'

They came in.

'Please sit down.'

They sat down.

'Would you like some tea?'

There was panic in their eyes.

'Tea?' I repeated.

They decided, after enquiring glances at one another, that it was more correct to refuse.

'Mister, mister, can I touch your pistol?'

Julia stood in the door in her pink nightdress, her big eyes fastened on the soldier.

'Sure,' he said involuntarily.

Before he could recant she was sitting on his knee getting her first lesson in ballistics.

'I'm sorry but I just can't leave her on her own,' I said to the fur coat.

He scratched his head.

'It looks like you can't and yet you must. Blast it, I wasn't told about the child.'

'I can drop her off at a friend's place. Can you take us there?'

'To hell with it, I will.'

◊

The night is pitch black. I'm driven through a tunnel towards the Mouth of Hell.

(You're overdoing it now.)

(It's easy for you to talk.)

I can't see anything. Past and future fall away from me. It doesn't matter any more that I was loved by five men or that I brought a child into the world or that I wrote a prize-winning doctorate in psychology. I won't have any more adventures or listen to Julia's bedtime stories. I will end like my father, swept from the ottoman, my work in tatters.

Will Julia think of me as I think of him? Will she inherit my fear?

It was long past curfew when we set out. As we approached the dreary towers of Kurbanow, all dirty-green and crumbling like blocks of rotten cheese, I grew anxious. Which one was the Janickis'? In daylight or at night they all looked exactly alike. We drove around in circles, bumping over piles of snow and creeping into culs-de-sac. The fur coat was getting impatient.

'It looks like, how to say it . . . ?'

'Hold on,' I beseeched him. 'I know what to do! I always come here by bus, so if you drop me at the bus stop I'll find my way on foot.'

The fur coat sighed, asked the soldier to find the bus stop and then escorted Julia and me to the Janickis' place.

◊

I thought that Julia would cry and cling to me but she was cool and composed. Really, if they were serious about averting future trouble, they should have arrested her and not me.

'That's a brave little girl you have,' said the fur coat as we walked back to the bus stop.

After about ten minutes I realized that I had got it mixed up again and that we were heading in the wrong direction. So we doubled back and walked straight into the arms of a patrol.

'Your documents,' demanded a pimpled young sergeant.

'I don't have my documents,' I said. 'This gentleman took them.'

'Your documents,' the sergeant turned to the fur coat.

'All the documents are in the car,' stammered the fur coat. 'I'm in the process of interning this lady and, how to say it?, we just got lost.'

The sergeant looked at me for confirmation.

What was I to say? Frankly I didn't much care whether I was arrested in the process of internment or interned in the process of arrest. I felt like sitting down in the snow and crying for Julia and Feliks and myself.

Just then our car arrived. The soldier had got tired of waiting for us and had begun a search. The men agreed among themselves on who should possess the booty and saluted one another.

We drove off again.

I was thrown into a cellar which stank like Lazarus' socks. There were three other women there, an open WC and two benches on which to sleep. Two of the women were crying.

The one who cried the most was Beata, a glamorous secretary to some Solidarity leader in Kozle. She was due to take her driving test the following day. She cried and cried because if she missed the test she would lose her deposit. Every now and then she dabbed her eyes, fluffed up her hair-do and smoothed down her angora sweater. She was the kind of woman who would try to catch a glimpse of her coiffure and her eye shadow in the polished metal of the blade before losing her head to a guillotine.

Next in the crying stakes was a woman with spiky hair who cleaned the Solidarity offices. They arrested her because she was on the list of employees. Her name was Rozalia and she heaved like a sick porcupine between her bits and pieces of folk wisdom.

'If you clean a bank that doesn't make you a million-aire. If you clean a Solidarity office it doesn't make you a troublemaker, right?' And she shook all her quills.

Their lamentations liberated my own long-suppressed tears. I hadn't cried since Barnaba's investigation and now I found myself bewailing all the years since: the loss of Damian, of Aleksander and of Feliks, the loss of Julia, of this New Year and God only knew how many years of punishment yet to come.

The three of us sat on the cold benches swaying and sobbing until it seemed that there were stalagtites hanging from our eyes and that we would carry these crystalline growths to our graves.

Dorota refused to join in our wailing. She just sat on the floor in the lotus position and bit her fingernails. She looked like George Sand in her black waistcoat and black velvet trousers, her face hidden in a mahogany page-boy hair-cut. She had an intensity and inner concentration that scared me. Women like her walk over corpses to reach their goal.

'Why don't you cry?' asked Rozalia accusingly. 'Are you a spy or what?'

'No. I'm an actress.'

'Jesus,' said Rozalia. 'You could at least pretend. What are you in for?'

'I was at this farewell party for a guy who was waiting to be interned. They came for him in the middle of the party. When we kicked up a stink about it they took the rest of us as well for rude behaviour.'

Her clear unemotional account only deepened our grief and self-pity. She just sat there and bit her fingernails and we cried for her.

'What do you think they'll do to us?' asked Beata.

'You know what they did to Mrs Kulka?' said Rozalia. 'She came out in 1967 with . . .'

'Don't tell me!' cried Beata. 'I don't want to hear!'

'Sons of bitches!' said Rozalia. 'You know, first they practise it on us before trying it on their wives. For example they . . . '

'Stop!' cried Beata.

A guard stood at the door, waving Declarations of Loyalty to the General.

'Who's going to be first to rejoin the human race?'

Beata stopped crying, grabbed a Declaration, signed it without reading it and was immediately released.

We gaped in astonishment.

'Who'd have thought that joining the human race would be such a simple business?' said Rozalia.

'Nothing is simpler than a pact with the devil,' said Dorota.

Dorota, Rozalia and I stayed on in prison for a while. On New Year's Eve, over flour soup, we talked about carnival dresses and the men we had danced with at New Year balls. Rozalia wondered what it would be like to be a man and dance with an erection. Was it painful? And what happened if you ejaculated? She told us the story of a man who taped his penis to his thigh to keep it quiet. Later he was seen leaving the dance floor hopping on one leg like . . . well, like . . . none of us knew a bird which hopped with one leg at right angles to the other.

(A fuckbird?)

(Very good. A fuckbird.)

The Great Spotted Fuckbird appeared in our cell a few days later with a sheaf of Declarations of Loyalty.

'Brezhnev is dead,' he said matter-of-factly.

'Now ladies, who's next to rejoin the human race?'

'If Brezhnev is dead we can all go home,' said Rozalia with fake enthusiasm. 'There'll be an amnesty. There's always an amnesty when one of those gangsters dies.'

'Of course,' jeered Dorota. 'And then we can all go back to building the bright future.'

Rozalia ignored her.

'As God is my witness my hand signs this but I don't.'

(Just like Dev.)

(Like who?)

And so Rozalia signed and joined the human race.

I was left in the cell with Dorota, who was growing more and more militant. I wasn't. I was dirty and scratchy and dazed with sleeplessness. If Dorota could resist her surroundings I found myself being defined by them. The mere fact of being a prisoner made me feel guilty.

Once, when I was sitting on the loo, a guard burst in on me. What was I to do? Stand up? It was silly to stand up with my knickers round my knees. Yell at him? A woman can't really yell at a man while sitting on a loo. I felt defiled.

When it happened to Dorota she just told the guard to piss off. She had a more integrated personality than I. She consumed all the energy and vitality in the cell so that there was nothing left for me.

The next time the Great Spotted Fuckbird came in looking

for applicants to join humanity I said guiltily to Dorota: 'I can't support the cause any more. I have to support myself. Don't you think it's altogether too much for an unmarried mother to fight against communism?'

'Cut the bullshit and sign.'

So I signed and got out.

Dorota refused and was taken to an atrocious internment camp on the Russian border where she got dysentry. She had never struggled for anything before. It was in jail that she discovered that she had beliefs and that she was ready to die for them.

Intermission Four

On Tea, Sex and Martial Law

On December 13, 1981 the extraterrestrials detected a new black hole in the cosmos. It emitted no light and it continued to contract and densify at an alarming rate, as is the case with such phenomena.

Not since the spontaneous combustion of the Dragon in the days of Krak had our city come so forcefully to the attention of the Watchers From On High.

After the great gravitational collapse Krakovians were flung into a dead zone, a torque in time and space from which there was no escape. At one moment it seemed that we were in 1981, at another we were back in 1863 or even — perish the thought — at the latter end of the age of stone and bone. Wherever we were, we had been there before and, it seemed, we would be there again.

On the one hand, one could certainly claim that Kraków was still Kraków, a crumbling Renaissance city in Eastern Europe on the River Vistula, 53°8'N and 8°57'W. It was linked to the world by road, rail and the Yalta Agreement. On the other hand, it was no longer there. It was disconnected from the rest of Europe, free-floating in a space of its own. As such it was hardly of interest to anybody except philanthropists and philatelists.

Only a revived medieval cartography, with its blank spaces inscribed 'Here be Comrades' could chart the slippage between worlds.

As one might expect, the denizens of the black hole contracted and densified with their city. They went to work but found there was nothing to do. They went to shops and found there was nothing to buy. They went to the library and found nothing but historical romances about Teutonic knights that they had all read long long ago in their childhood. They switched on the television and found to their amazement that they were in some Latin American dictatorship where hatchet-faced presenters read the news in military uniform. So they switched off again and returned to King Jagiello and the Battle of Grünwald of 1410.

Overnight the most innocuous places – cafés, cinemas, theatres, urinals – became pathogenic zones. They were either under observation or closed down since they were potential sites for conspiracy against compulsory contraction and densification.

Everything was still present and yet absent. The House-wives' Association, the Football Club, the Writers' Union, the Fellowship of Father Klimuszko, and the Wawel Radiosthetic Investigative Bureau, Solidarity – they were there. And yet they weren't.

Is it any wonder that, as a refuge from this giddy quantum leap, Krakovians turned to the only durable thing in the world? Besides, what were they to do after eleven o'clock, with everything closed or suspended?

They went to bed. Electricians, academics, plumbers, morticians, cinema projectionists, layabout journalists and unemployed actors, they all went to bed and rediscovered their genitalia.

The streets were full of pregnant women and puling infants. Holy Mass was clogged with baptisms at which the officiating clergy encouraged their flock to increase and multiply even further. And so they increased like potato beetles and devoured everything in their path.

To all outward appearances we were a modern society: we had a bureaucracy, abstract art and washing machines. But in truth all the energy of the people went into foraging for food, performing the deed of life and cajoling God, His Angels and Saints. We were once again a neolithic tribe reduced to fornication, food-gathering and ritual incantations.

(But what about the tea?)

Adventure Eleven

In which Faustyna Experiences Multiple Betrayals

Reasonable people claim we can live together with the monster. We only have to avoid sudden movements, sudden speech, the poet said. *If there is a threat, assume the form of a rock or a leaf. Listen to wise nature recommending mimicry. That we breath shallowly, pretend we aren't there.*

After betraying the revolution I tried to be reasonable and I assumed the protective colouring of the shrunken world around me. The university was closed so I spent most of my time at home or in queues. I allowed the day's tedium and the night's vacuity to silt up inside me. I even abandoned my jazzy waistcoat and peacock earrings.

This tactical drabness alarmed Julia.

'Are you old now, Mammy,' she asked one day, 'and will you soon die?'

'Eat up your nothing soup.'

Nothing soup was brewed from stale bread, lots of garlic, salt and water.

She put down her spoon and gave me a basilisk glance. Her despotism was in inverse proportion to her father's shyness, as if to right an imbalance in nature.

'Very well, it's like this. I'm not dying but I'm short of meaning. Jesus, how to explain it?'

'Why do you have to say Jesus all the time?'

'What about Jeepers Creepers, then? Is that allowed in this house?'

Julia nodded.

'Where was I?'

Where was I indeed? I had to find something to say that would hold our world together long enough to enable Julia to do her homework and me to queue for bread.

'Remember the way the tide came in and went away out again when we were at the seaside? It's the same with the meaning of things. One day you wake up and the meaning has leaked from everything, even the bed-clothes. When that happens you mustn't lose your head. Because however far out it goes it's sure to come in again. Just now the meaning is out.'

'Where is it?'

'I don't know. I can't even see it on the horizon.'

'Then how do you know it's there at all?'

'I can smell it.'

'I don't believe you.'

I didn't believe it myself. I was sinking. It was mainly not to be bested by Julia that I went for the Grand Design Theory. It could justify even the existence of cancer cells and rabies.

'Look here. If we're thirsty there's water in the world to quench our thirst. If we're hungry there's food out there somewhere. Why else would we be hungry? If we need meaning there must be meaning, the same as salt. It's simple. The mistake is to think that it must be there all the time.'

'But for some people it is there all the time.'

'Who, for example?'

'General Jaruzelski. Or Princess Diana.'

'One day it will go out for them too.'

'No,' said Julia with finality. 'For them the tide is always in. I'm sure.'

The tide came trickling in, runnel by runnel, at the end of March. I met a man who had met a man who had met a man who said the underground wanted someone to talk to the workers and to the leaders who were still at large. They needed to find out how much life was left in the movement. I was the right man for the job they said. I had all the addresses and the contacts.

The idiocy of the underground life. Four generations had trembled in cellars, souterrains and haylofts, so preoccupied with themselves that they had forgotten the existence of normal places like Galway Bay in Connaught or Private Bay in New Zealand. Worse, they had forgotten how to talk straight and had lost one another in indecipherable codes.

Willy nilly, I continued the tradition to the fifth generation.

I'm supposed to go to Piastowska Street number so-and-so with my questionnaires. When the woman comes to the door I must say: 'I'm just making some ginger cake. Could you loan me a couple of eggs till Friday?'

And I'm not supposed to hand over anything until she says, 'I'm sorry, I ate my last egg for breakfast.'

An hour later my head is swimming. Maybe it isn't ginger cake at all, maybe it's sponge cake? I know I'm supposed to ask for eggs, but how many? Half a dozen seems excessive. And when was I to have them back? Friday or Monday or Saturday?

I say to the woman: 'I'm very sorry, ma'am, but I'm making this cake and I'm not sure if it's a cheese cake or a sponge cake. But anyway, I need some eggs and I'll let you have them back as soon as I can.'

The woman looks at me uncertainly, as well she might. She says: 'Could you come back again some other time when you know what you want?'

And then I have to go through the whole rigmarole again, get a new address, a new password, write it down, lose the bit of paper and mix it all up: eggs, cakes, dates and codes.

I suffered from a permanent nervous breakdown because I never knew whether I had used the right password or if I had given the results of my research to the right contact. I cursed my absentmindedness until the day I met a man who called himself 'Marek'.

I was sitting in the Journalists' Club, having my usual coffee and rollmops, when a black-browed, strong-jawed, corduroy-clad man strolled by. He stopped by my table and said, 'Excuse me madam, have you heard the church bells ringing?'

'No, I haven't. Why?'

He kept on looking at me with an eager question mark in his eyes.

Another code, blast it. What was the response?

'I'm terribly forgetful,' I said. 'I know there's an answer to that one but I'm damned if I can remember it.'

He smiled.

'Never mind. I knew it must be you. There's only one woman with such titian hair in the whole of Kraków.'

Before I knew what was happening he had taken over the table and me. He was one of those men who could create a mood with a chuckle or a wink or a sweep of his hand. A mood of expectancy. He held it glowing between us like a cloud of candyfloss.

'What's your name?'

'Let's just say Marek. I'll be your link man from now on. You can just relax and do your research and pass it over to me.'

We met in cafés, drank rowanberry vodka, conspired and flirted. Stronger than Siberian ginseng, than ground rhinoceros horn, stronger even than the glands of musk deer, a blend of conspiracy and flirtation is the most potent aphrodisiac.

Under the table I slipped him the results of my latest research. Over the table we exchanged coy smiles, lingering glances, extravagant passwords and quizzes.

What's thirty centimetres long, spotted and hangs in front of an asshole?

Answer: Brezhnev's tie.

Or: What's the difference between democracy and socialist democracy?

Answer: The same as the difference between a chair and an electric chair?

(Why did the Galwayman go to the Orient?)

(I don't know. I give up.)

(Because he thought Fuck-ing was a town in China.)

And so on and so forth.

I wanted to find out his real name, what he did for a living and whether he was married. He always managed to parry my questions with a joke or a Casablanca smile that showed a full set of even teeth. He was witty but there was something raw and unfinished about him, maybe even something stupid, despite the blasé cigarette that hung nostalgically from his lips. When I probed him I thought I found under the lacquered shell the squirming stupidity of a peasant.

But I set all of that aside.

Once again – was it because it was springtime and the cherries were in blossom – I began to fantasize about how Julia, Marek and I would register on the astral lenses of the extraterrestrials. The extraterrestrials were my litmus test for the reality of things.

I plodded on with my questions and came to relish Marek's brassy evasions the way one might relish the wiles of a good poker player. Until one day, heedlessly, I hadn't even planned it, simply puzzled by something he had said, I asked: 'What are your politics, as a matter of interest?'

'I'm a rightist revisionist,' he replied without a smidge of irony.

No pearly teeth this time or raised eyebrows.

'You must be joking. Tell me you're joking.'

He was genuinely puzzled. 'I thought we were all rightist revisionists?'

So that's how it was. I tore at myself, trammelled in a spider's web. Stray words and glances fell into a pattern. 'Rightist revisionist' was a term used only by the secret police when they talked about the opposition. I instantly imagined a training session for new recruits, fresh from Pszczyna and Jastrzebie, at which the instructor said, ' . . . and if you are asked about your political views, you say you're a rightist revisionist.'

Marek scrupulously wrote it all down in the same neat copybook as he had earlier noted a series of jokes that might come in handy on different occasions. Nothing was left to chance. What is thirty centimetres long, spotted and hangs in front of an asshole?

Answer: Brezhnev's/Jaruzelski's/Jaroszewicz's/Honecker's tie.

'I can hear the bells ringing all right,' I said.

I shouldn't have said it. I shouldn't have stood up

abruptly like that with murder in my eyes. I shouldn't have stumbled out in a hurry, bumping into everything. I should have known better.

There was a blizzard in my head as I walked towards Sukiennice. It wasn't very encouraging to learn that I was flirting with an informer and had handed over to him all my research on Solidarity. Now I was done for. I had signed a pledge of allegiance and at the same time widened my anti-state activities. I had forced myself through the hell of conspiracy and then blurted out my results to an informer.

I had to get out of Kraków before they came for me for the second time.

Out of the blizzard an apparition emerged. I saw her striding towards the Dominikan Church on thin stick legs with her satchel on her back.

What was she doing here? She shouldn't be in this part of town at all.

Stealthily I followed her to find out who she was betraying. I knew by the resolute way she entered the church that she had been there many times before. She made her way up the aisle and turned to a side altar. Tiny and vulnerable she paused beneath the baroque splendour of Our Lady the Merciful. She lit two candles and knelt down.

Who had taught her to pray?

Who told her what to do in church?

I hadn't even baptized her.

I moved closer to have a better look. She wasn't praying. Her hands weren't even joined. She was kneeling at the prie-dieu, gazing intently at the socratic face of the Virgin.

So Julia had found herself another mother. She was cajoling her with candles. Was one of them for my wretched soul?

Adventure Twelve

In which Faustyna is Tempted by Mephisto

Julia looked festive with her orange and green rucksack on her back and a blue bandana across her brow. I told her we were going on a magical mystery tour, the same as in the Beatles' song, and she was as chirpy and excited as a goldfinch. Just before we left she furrowed her brow: 'Have you told my teacher, Mammy? I have a maths test on Monday.'

How pert and prim she was! How eager to be examined! I felt, not for the first time, a pang of adolescent envy. For her, everything still had its proper time and place. There were standards against which to measure things. She did not yet know how friable our world was.

'Don't worry. I'll explain to your teacher and you'll get your A-plus, never fear. Now we'd better go.'

We didn't get very far. Instead of a taxi, an unmarked car with two UBEKS in leather jackets drew up.

'Where do you think you're going?' one of them asked, opening the back door.

'It's none of your business . . . sir,' I said, trapped between defiance and resignation.

'You're coming with us,' said the other. 'Get in with your brat.'

He stank of garlic. I called him Rancid. The other one had a sly, lecherous grin. I called him Randy. They were rough and aggressive. Julia's face was white with fear. I had to help her off with her rucksack.

'Take it easy,' I said. 'These two gentlemen are simply nervous.'

'What are you yapping about,' yelled Rancid. 'Nervous my arse.'

Julia cringed. She had never heard anybody yelling at me before.

'What are they going to do to us, Mammy?'

'Nothing. It's all a show. Don't take them seriously.'

'You'd better be serious this time,' said Randy looking at me in his driving mirror.

'No we won't,' said Julia.

Randy and Rancid guffawed.

At the police station I clutched her little hand till it hurt her.

'Don't make a scene,' said Rancid. 'We'll look after the brat. You come with me.'

I let go of Julia's hand.

'I'm not leaving my Mammy,' said Julia, with her arms akimbo.

An ancient hysteria swelled in me. My mother's hysteria that I hated. If I unleash it now, Julia will never forget it. She will forget our arrest but she will never forget the self-indulgent savagery of a mother's love.

'We'll go on our trip another day,' I said as calmly as I could. 'I promise. Be a good girl. Follow the gentleman.'

Julia's magical mystery tour ended up in a reformatory for juvenile criminals. She was given paper and crayons and she drew tanks and fire engines.

'Have you ever met a man called Feliks Wolicki?' asked the Warden for the third time.

She didn't answer. She drew more and more tanks, sinking her crayon deeper and deeper into the cheap paper.

'I want my Mammy,' she said eventually.

'Your Mammy is interned because she did silly things.'

'You did silly things. You declared martial law.'

I was led into a large office where I was left waiting for hours and hours. Rheumy desks, phones rimed with dried male sweat and spittle, filing cabinets swollen with our meticulously catalogued transgressions, grey gun-metal walls, frosted glass windows, the floor flayed alive by hobnail boots.

They made me feel like dirt clogged under a fingernail.

Once in a while a policeman came in, made a phone call or rifled through files and left. And these entrances, these prolonged phone calls to the wives, these casual reshufflings of paper, were so innocent and yet so diabolic. They simply pretended that I wasn't there and I felt my substance thinning out.

'There were strikes and strikes and nobody wanted to work,' said the Warden.

'My mother wanted to.'

'That's not what I hear. Besides, I don't think she's a good mother. She doesn't look after you properly, does she? No. She spends most of her time writing bad things about the government.'

'It's the government started it all. The government was shooting at the workers.'

'How do you know that?'

'From the song.'

'What song?'

'The song about Janek Wisniewski. Everybody knows that song.'

'I don't.'

At ten o'clock the door swung open and Sherlock Holmes strode in, followed by a cringing squab who clicked his heels.

'At last, Colonel. We were waiting for you, Colonel. How was your journey, sir? Can I get you a cup of coffee?'

'Coffee would be fine. Two coffees.'

Aha, I thought. A VIP. I knew immediately what they wanted from me.

'Miss Faustyna,' cried the Colonel, putting his bony hand on my shoulder, 'what are you doing here? You were supposed to be in Warsaw!'

He smelled of something piquant which made me hungry. Old Spice.

'I hope they didn't find anything incriminating in your luggage?'

'I'm afraid I don't understand,' I said in a ladylike manner to match his tweedy hauteur.

'Let me put it to you this way, then. Your internment is a misunderstanding. The police here are a bit on the zealous side.'

I was sure I had seen him before somewhere.

'Miss Faustyna, we have an entirely different future planned for you. We are not interested in Solidarity. Frankly, we couldn't care less about the underground. It's all going to crumble to pieces in the next few months. We think in terms of decades, twenty, thirty years.'

I knew that from time immemorial the only two institutions that had the cheek to think in terms of decades were the Catholic Church and the Intelligence Service.

So Julia stood up and sang the song about Janek Wisniewski.

> *Dzisiaj milicja uzyla broni*
> *Dzielniesmy stali*
> *Celnie rzucali*
> *Janek Wisniewski padl.*

(Won't you translate it for me?)
(There isn't time.)

'You sing very nicely,' said the Warden, 'but the song has got it all wrong. It's the workers who started it. They threw stones at the police.'

'They didn't.'

'They did, I assure you. Ask your mother.'

'I'm very sorry to meet you in these circumstances. I was looking forward to a pleasant chat in pleasant surroundings.'

'Now I remember you,' I said. 'You were at the Solidarity Conference in Gdańsk with "Accredited Journalist" on your lapel.'

Holmes swallowed the affront. He hit back quietly.

'We know all about you. We know about your project and who you have seen.'

'Yes, I saw almost everybody worth seeing.'

'Exactly. We've noticed that you have an excellent rapport with men. You like adventure, don't you? This nonsense you're involved in, these theories of yours, they're all, excuse my expression, infantile. By the way, why are you involved in it at all? You're not the type. What's in it for you?'

That threw me. Well, I'll throw him.

'It's to help me meet interesting men.'

He smiled instantly.

'Not bad. You've got the hang of these things already.'

I squirmed under his approval. Was I really interested in 'Why Solidarity and Where Does it Lead To?'?

'I'm proposing a real game,' he went on. 'An interesting game with lots at stake.'

The squab brought coffee, which gave me the time to pull myself together.

'You'll understand,' I said, 'that I can't concentrate just now. I can't think of anything but my daughter. I have to have an assurance that she is safe and well looked after.'

'I'm sorry about what's happened,' said the Colonel. 'Of course I'd very much like to help you. But, as you see, I'm only a guest here. I can't meddle very much with the internal affairs of these gentlemen.' He turned to the squab. 'Unless, of course, you'd let us use your phone for a few minutes?'

'Of course, of course, Colonel,' said the squab. 'I'll get you a line.'

'If I intervene,' the Colonel leaned towards me, 'I must have some guarantee that you won't leave me stranded.'

I decided that I'd better show him my hand because he was so much more adept at the game of human poker.

'I can't give you any guarantee. I can only promise that I'll talk to you if you let me talk to my daughter.'

I waited a long time to be put through to Julia.

'Mama, who started it all?' she burst out. 'Was it the government or the workers?'

'Are you all right, Little Pumpkin?'

'Tell me who started it.'

'Where are you and what are they doing to you?'

'The Warden said it was the workers but I said it was the government.'

'You were right. Did they give you your dinner?'

'Yes. I knew it was the government and I told him so.'

'Granny will collect you in a few days. Be brave.'

I sang him the song about Janek Wisniewski,' she said proudly. 'Imagine! he didn't even know it! They are stupid like you always say.'

The phone clicked and went dead. I knew that Julia was fine and in her favourite element. She was having an argument.

'Now let's get down to business,' said the Colonel.

'One last thing. I need to ring my mother to tell her to pick up Julia.'

Holmes sighed.

'You strike a hard bargain. You'd better deliver the goods.'

The thought of talking to my mother made me more nervous than the thought of continuing the conversation with the Colonel. I prepared a sentence in my head:

'Mama, this is Faustyna, I've just been interned. Julia is with the police. Can you collect her?'

It wasn't the best way of starting a conversation with my mother after not seeing her for a year.

'Faustyna, what are you telling me, where are you, what's going on?'

'Would you collect Julia from the police as soon as possible?'

I could hear her beginning to sob.

'Just shut up for once and do it, OK?'

'Are you all right?'

'Promise me to collect Julia and look after her. She has an exam on Monday.'

'Have they given you anything to eat?'

'Sorry about all this, Mammy. I'll be away for some time.'

I put down the phone to cut off the flow of Belorussian tears and abuse.

'My dear Miss Faustyna, you will be released tomorrow if we can come to an agreement.'

'Go on.'

'We'd like to collaborate with you in the future.'

'What do you have in mind?'

'Adventures, as I said. Lots of foreign travel. No shortage of money or good places to stay. With the odd task thrown in of course.'

'What task?'

'That we can discuss later.'

'You mean spying, don't you?'

'No, not at all. Building up the right contacts and connections perhaps? Don't be reductive about it. You've seen too many silly movies, my dear. These days it's more of a public relations exercise.'

'Why me?'

'You have the right profile. We want only the best. Well-groomed, attractive women with good communication skills.' He seemed to be quoting from a minute or an internal memo. Then more informally. 'Somebody with a bit of dash. Somebody who can get along well with men.'

Switzerland. You can send me to Switzerland. Nothing very extravagant to begin with. Near Lausanne perhaps – clean country wines and cheeses, millionaire recluses masturbating in lakeside villas. Me straying on the terrace in a simple black cocktail dress and getting on well with men. They are burning old branches in the vineyards above us. You explain everything to me, all the local customs. My, but we are getting along! Yes, why don't you tell me about your arms export business to the Middle East? I know some people in Warsaw.

Mephisto looked at me with friendly anticipation.

(Hold on. Why Mephisto all of a sudden?)

(You know how it is. First he was more of a Holmes, then he turned into Mephisto.)

'What alternatives do I have if I say no?' I asked.

'Well, with all your files and this so-called research of yours, you'll get at least five years.'

'Five years!'

'At least. Now I hope we can reach a reasonable solution.'

◊

We were both fellow artists, were we not? Mephisto's head, like mine, was crammed with plots, dramatic climaxes and last-minute reversals.

The girl on the terrace who provided end-user certificates had sex appeal. She would never know anything about bursting bodies in Kabul or in the Gambia. She would go from party to party in her black cocktail dress and talk about Roland Barthes or minimalist painting. There would be nothing to connect her to slaughter or abasement. She would be even more removed from destruction than the pilots who dropped bombs on invisible cities.

Was there a reasonable compromise, something in the spirit of the English parliamentary tradition?

I took a deep breath of the stale, sickly air.

'OK. For me a reasonable solution is as follows. I don't want to have anything to do with you. Let's ignore the moral aspect and speak of technicalities. It's obvious that martial law can't last for five years. Once it's lifted, I'll be out. But if I do business with you it'll be for life.'

Mephisto looked at me with a mixture of disappointment and pity.

'I thought you would be more sensible.'

'I have my limitations.'

'Aa, we know why you're so saucy,' the squab broke in. 'We read some interesting things you wrote to your little Feliks.'

We had returned to the tangible.

'Is this Peeping Tom a friend of yours?' I asked Mephisto.

Adventure Thirteen

Hardly an Adventure since Much of Faustyna's Life is Spent in Parenthesis

There were six echelons of people in our internment camp and each of them kept an eye on the others according to a hierarchy of watchmen.

At the bottom of the hierarchy were common criminals – thieves and forgers – who worked in the kitchens and prepared food for the rest of us. Everybody kept an eye on the criminals.

Next came the political internees, men and women together, for ours was the only mixed camp in the country.

We were watched by the prison guards. Some of the prison guards were former members of Solidarity so they couldn't be trusted an inch.

The criminals, the internees and the guards were watched by soldiers of the regular army. The soldiers were not reliable either: most of them were not yet twenty and their parents were on different sides of the political divide. Their morale was very low, they fought viciously with one another and sulked around the camp with bruised faces and black eyes.

Adventure Thirteen

The criminals, the internees, the guards and the soldiers were watched by the Voluntary Reserve of the Civil Militia. Still, ideologically speaking, the Reservists were not the brightest or the best-informed.

So at the top of the hierarchy of watchmen were the Security Police. They had to watch over the militia, the soldiers, the guards, the internees and the criminals. They were the true patriots.

We were interned in what had once been a seaside sanatorium. It was comfortable, had bright airy rooms and there were clean crisp sheets on the beds. Locked doors and windows were the only inconvenience.

We spent days, weeks, months, years talking, smoking and planning for the future. We were the Social Science Department of the City University of Limbo, well insulated from reality, addicted to paradigms and phantasmagoria, abrasive in our hysteria and powerlessness.

We could have gone on like that for a hundred years, talking, smoking, calculating, arguing, comparing models, committing suicide over models, and it wouldn't have made a sparrow's fart of a difference to anything.

But for the real workers of the world, who were used to getting up at five o'clock and rushing to the shipyards, the camp was hell. They still got up at dawn but they had nowhere to go. So they paced back and forth along the endless corridors like a procession of the damned, and kept the rest of us awake.

◊

I refuse to describe life in the internment camp. To have endured its tedium once is enough. Why re-live and re-create the vacuity and the boredom? Fine if it were the vacuity of the English aristocracy or the boredom of the French bourgeoisie or even the paralysis of the Irish intelligentsia. But who in their right mind wants to read about the existential horror of Eastern European intellectuals?

Better bracket the whole thing the way we were bracketed in the camps. Better leave a few pages blank.

(It's been done before. Come on, something must have happened.)

(Of course something happened. Something shameful, what else?)

One day of many days, the same day but different, a man came up to me. We were, as usual, pacing along a corridor until we reached the NO EXIT sign and then back again until the next NO EXIT. A man whose face I knew from press photographs passed by several times. Each time he looked at me intensely. He was like a bullock preparing to charge a red rag and then, at the last moment, backing off. Finally he attacked.

'I have a question. Have you ever had a judge in your family?'

'Oh yes. My father's brother, Robert Falk, was a prosecutor.'

'In Lublin, right?'

'In Lublin. Why?'

'Walk with me and I'll tell you.'

'When I was ten, in 1947, my father was arrested. We didn't hear about him for months. In the end my mother got a letter from the Public Prosecutor. She cried when she read it. Days and nights she cried. I stole the letter to find out what it was all about. The letter said my father got fifteen years in jail for publishing some brochure or other. The letter was signed Robert Falk. I never saw my father again.'

'I'm sorry.'

I was helpless and defensive as a hornless cow. I'd forgotten all about Uncle Robert. The man was going to force me to remember.

'Have you heard how many Polish war veterans he executed? People who had risked their lives to fight the Germans, people who had been tortured in German camps?'

'No.'

'Good for you.'

His eyes were fastened on my face as if he were scanning me for an executioner's genes.

I looked away to escape his hatred. Or perhaps it wasn't hatred? Perhaps it was an inherited despair that he wanted to share with me?

'Well, well,' I tried to mollify him. 'And to think that we are meeting one another in this camp now! How strange is the fate of the Poles!'

He didn't smile or nod his head.

'From what I heard this Robert Falk was a Jew.'

'That's right,' I said quickly, 'my family is partly Jewish. Robert was my father's brother all right but they quarrelled and hardly ever saw one another.' I was backpedalling as fast as I could.

'Is he still alive?'

'To tell the truth I don't know.'

'I see,' he said softly and walked away.

He planted suspicion and guilt in me. I had never thought of Uncle Robert as a monster. He married a woman who called him You Lousy Jew all his life. His children also called him a Lousy Jew. After the war he returned with many of his kind from Russia and got down to the task of eliminating counter-revolutionaries.

Where was he now, this very unhappy, very good communist?

And I? Where was I, a very unhappy, very bad dissident?

Intermission Five

Feliks's Censored Letter to Faustyna from Internment Camp

My dear Faustyna,

xxxxxxxxxxxxxxxxxxxxxxxxxxxxxxxxxxxxxxxxxxxxxxxxxxx all these months. I hope you're well as I am here. What a pity we never crossed the bridge on the xxxxxxx together. Did you ever get the bucket back? I told them to return the bucket when the xxxxxx finally confirmed that I lived where I said I did. My days here are dull but the nights are full of xxxxx and xxxxxxxxx xxxxxxxxxxxxxxx in your flannelette pyjamas with the ladybirds. I wish my xxxx were sixty centimetres long and could curl up inside you like a cat.

Speaking of animals, something strange is happening to me here. I find myself standing on one leg when peeling potatoes or talking to people. But it's not just the leg, I'm afraid. My head is tilted to one side and my shoulders are hunched up. I try to straighten myself out but again and again I find that the toes of my left foot curl and I discover to my amazement that I'm standing with one leg tucked under the other. I think I'm turning into a heron. You're the psychologist, maybe you know the name of my pathology and its cure. Even as I write I find myself straining upwards and unwilling to stand on my own two feet. It's very uncomfortable and I wish it would pass. Am I going mad? YES!! [censor's note]

Do write an explanation to me. As a heron would I ever be able to xxxxxx xxx xxx xxx???

Yours forever.

F.

Adventure Fourteen

In which Faustyna Lives in Two Hearts of Darkness

'At the stroke of midnight the door swung open and the General strode in, followed by a sleazy, slimy, spooky squab. The General's chest was absolutely tiled with medals: Virtuti Militari, the Order of Lenin, Builder of the People's Republic, War Combatant, the lot.

' "Miss Faustyna," he said, kissing my hand. "What on earth are you doing here? You're supposed to be in Warsaw." '

'They were trying to trap you, Mammy,' said Julia. 'Did he ask you about me?'

'He said you were the hardest nut that they ever had to crack.'

Julia giggled at her own fortitude.

' "I'm sorry to put you to so much trouble," said the General, opening a bottle of cognac. "You are a very special woman and we have a very special mission for you." '

'He was trying to make you drunk, Mammy. Or maybe it was drugged? What did you say again?'

'Well, as I told you, I said to the General: Go stuff your mission up your jersey!'

Julia keeled over on the bed.

'But he wouldn't give up. He offered me money, cars, a private helicopter, trips to the Bahamas, diamonds and rubies, servants and silk dresses. I wouldn't budge. My daughter Julia and I are not for sale, I said. In that case, madam – and here the General stood up like so – in that case you'll be shot at dawn. Come on now, go to sleep Little Pumpkin.'

'No. I want to hear how you forbade them to blindfold you before the firing squad.'

'You've already heard that story half a dozen times. I have a better idea: why don't we both reward ourselves tomorrow with a Napoleon cake and a nice cup of tea?'

I had spent a whole day telling and retelling Julia the story of my internment. I added a detail here, substituted a scene there, until we had jointly confected a fable that satisfied her need for a heroic mother and mine for a daughter's love.

At the end of our first day together, after a year's separation, Julia settled back contentedly into her pillow. Her green eyes were filled with something I had not seen before: tender admiration for me. Alleluia!

So far so good. Now to test the frontier of desire.

For months I had been dreaming of a cup of strong dark amber Yunnan tea with sugar and lemon. When I get this tea, I thought, I'll take it slowly, I'll savour every sip and drink it to the dregs. I won't care if the trumpets of Jericho are blaring over the city or if patriots are swinging from lampposts in the dawn rain, I'll just sit there unperturbed and drink it to the last drop.

Café Lux was open but cold and empty. It felt like a museum. The frescos on the wall, the cracked Doric columns, the empty tea canisters, the two waitresses in little black dresses and white pinafores, were merely on display to show how things were once upon a time and a long time ago.

In a faltering voice I asked for two glasses of tea with lemon and two Napoleons. Already I felt warm inside. Tea and Napoleons were moorings that fastened me to the good innocent past.

There was stony silence.

'I want milk in my tea,' piped up Julia

'Are you out of your mind?' shrieked the waitress.

'Have you heard that, Ivona?' She turned to the other woman. 'Her ladyship here wants tea and Napoleons.'

'Well, do you have coffee then?'

'She wants coffee as well!'

They looked to heaven.

'What do you have?'

'Plum compote, lemonade and vodka.'

'Lemonade and two compotes,' said Julia.

The waitress served us two bowls of brown liquid with two plums trying to disprove the Principle of Archimedes.

I didn't want plum compote. I could have had plum compote in jail. At Christmas. But we had to celebrate our reunion and my licence to roam the streets again and to choose my own meals. So we sat down in front of the fruit stew of freedom and smiled at one another.

We had come through.

We raised our spoons.

There was a sudden clank.

Julia looked aghast.

The spoons were chained to the table.

All the spoons, knives and forks in the café were chained to the tables. The chains were about thirty centimetres long. You had to bend low to eat.

'Let's go,' I heard myself saying.

As we left, the spectre of the evening crowd was milling in my head. I could see them through dense smoke, heads bent, chains rattling, feeding like convicts in the gulag.

Julia saw my desolation.

'Perhaps there are too many thefts,' she tried to console me.

But I couldn't free myself from the image of chained spoons. We had gone beyond being prisoners in our own country. We had become ingenious performers in a spectacle of self-abasement.

(By the way! Do you have any Yunnan tea?)

(Did you know that Yunnan tea is harvested by convicts in Chinese concentration camps?)

(So: I like prisoner's tea and you like prisoner's stories. Make the tea and I'll tell you the rest.)

Outside the café I bumped into a soft bosom.

'Faustyna!'

I didn't recognize her.

'Don't you remember me?' she cried.

'No.'

She bulged like a turnip in an expensive blue coat. Her head grew, chin upon chin, from an Arctic fox fur. The eyes were fat and tired, the helmet of lacquered hair had the consistency of sugar candy.

'We were together for two years. I'm Olivia.'

'Oh, my, but of course! You see we've just been to Lux and they have chained up the spoons . . . Forgive me, of course, Oblivia!'

'Is that your daughter?'

My daughter and your niece, I realized in a panic.

'What a divinely beautiful child!'

'Why don't you run along and count the pigeons?' I said to Julia before Aunt Oblivia searched out Damian in her.

Helter skelter, uneasily, we filled one another in on the previous ten years.

And Damian, what about Damian?

We tried to be warm but our eyes betrayed us. Hers said: Why haven't you changed? Why is it that you could be my teenage daughter?

Mine said: Good God. You who were the beauty among the beasts!

Our clocks were set to different times. Mine had stopped at the moment I entered the Europa Hotel to be deflowered. Hers followed Central European Standard Woman Time, a time that led inexorably to swollen babadom.

Damian was still in Kenya. He had married a Masai tribeswoman.

A Masai woman! There were tom-toms and goat test-icles for the betrothal feast. And Damian wreathed in orchids and bougainvillaea.

It was too remote, too far-fetched to inflict pain on me.

Oblivia had married a dentist, had three sons, lived here and there, did this and that and had recently been appointed a district court judge.

'I know what you're thinking,' she said quickly. 'Pigs might fly! But they've interned almost everybody so there were vacancies . . .'

'Congratulations,' I said half-heartedly.

She shrugged her shoulders. 'They pay me sweet fuck all. Fifteen thousand for being a judge? Fifteen thousand for sentencing people to swing? I'd be better off rearing chickens.'

She waved a pudgy hand. Her fingers were covered with Russian gold and rubies. There was something neuter about her, a vacancy, an absence, that she tried to cover with an excess of make-up, coiffure and rings.

She was never a human being and now she had ceased to be a woman.

But there was something of the old Oblivia left. She rooted in her shopping bag and pulled out a glass case with four exotic tropical butterflies, their gorgeous wings spread over pressed flowers.

'Look what I found at the new black market in Nowy Bierzanów. You simply won't believe the amount of stuff they have there! Everything from haunches of venison to Peruvian hats.'

We parted without exchanging addresses or phone numbers. We had tacitly agreed that it would be too perplexing to see one another again.

We were launched on two different trajectories around the same black hole.

There were no pyramids of papaya, mango, mandarin or pineapple, no fragrance of cinnamon, vanilla or coriander, no snake-charmers or sword-swallowers, or chalk-faced mime artists at the black market in Nowy Bierzanów.

There was a rank smell of naphthalene and rotting vegetables. In the most advantageous places were the autocratic vendors of eggs, butter, meat, coffee, tights and knickers. Soon they shall inherit the earth. In seven years' time they will drive round Kraków in white Mercedes with Fuck the Begrudgers on their lips.

Further back were the babas selling dried peas, nuts,

apples and strings of desiccated mushrooms, their faces old and wizened as their merchandise.

Scattered round the edges were the disgorged bowels of people's houses laid out on grey blankets or stacked higgledy-piggledy on the cobblestones. You shrank from the embarrassment of men and women with thoughtful faces exposing their heirlooms to appraising eyes in order to survive for another couple of months. You could almost hear the hum of desperate calculation going on in the heads of the women who traipsed from stall to stall to bargain for an egg or a piece of cheese costing a week's salary.

And you could hear me haggle doggedly over the price of an orange for Julia, an orange that wasn't too big or too small, too green or too ripe and that cost not more than three days' work at my Institute. An orange was a serious investment.

Then, cinematically, through the swirl of misery and mendacity, I homed in on it.

'Oh, look!' exclaimed Julia.

She had seen it at the same instant. A zebra mask. Striped white and black, elegant and impervious to the drabness all around.

A young man held it diffidently, as if to say, I know, I know; who in their right mind would want to buy an African mask in Kraków in this cruel spring of 1983?

We did. The minute we saw it we knew it was waiting for us. I could imagine it resplendent over my bed where Catholics hang crosses or sacred hearts.

A mandarin for Julia and a mask for me and we were happy, bankrupt and stricken with guilt at our extravagance.

'We can have nothing soup and potato pancakes for a few days,' said Julia.

Lovingly, she stroked the muzzle and the gaping nostrils as we elbowed our way out of the market. When we got free of the crowd I felt a tap on my shoulder.

'Excuse me, madam!' said a breathless voice in English. 'Excuse me!'

The man who spoke was not looking at me but at the zebra mask in Julia's hand. He couldn't take his eyes off it.

'Do you speak English?'

I nodded.

'Where did you find the mask?'

I pointed back to the market.

'I'm sorry to approach you in this way, but would you sell it to me?'

I shook my head.

'Ten dollars?'

'No!' said Julia.

He smiled.

'Very well, young lady. What about fifty dollars?'

'It's not for sale,' I said.

'Everything is for sale.'

His smile broadened showing the dimples on his cheeks.

'I really want this mask. Name your price.'

'What if I said a thousand dollars?'

I was struggling with my English and quaking at my impudence.

He was taken aback. But he was accustomed to greed.

'OK, if that's your price.'

He was tall and tanned and dressed in a white polo neck and an expensive tweed jacket. He had a strong muscular face softened by a smile that he wore as a talisman against the world.

'What's that man saying now?' asked Julia.

'He wants to give us lots and lots of money for the mask.'

Julia shook her head.

I turned to him. 'Why do you want it so very badly?'

He shrugged his shoulders. 'Because I like it.'

'Well, we like it too.'

'You mean you want more money? Come on! For a thousand dollars you could buy the whole bloody market. Besides, what use is an old African mask to you in . . . ?'

For a fleeting moment I was possessed by an old incubus. Hold fast to the ideological superiority of socialist man! Down with capitalist decadence!

But my ideological superiority faded on the instant. I wanted the mask just because, in these hard times it was decadent, superfluous to our needs, atavistic.

'Sorry,' I said.

He smiled again and shook his head.

Julia tugged at my sleeve.

'Tell the man that he can come to our apartment and look at it if he likes it so much.'

'What's she saying?'

'Nothing important.'

But Julia pulled her exercise book out of her satchel and wrote out our address for him in stilted calligraphy.

On the bus home she squeezed my hand and leaned against me as if to soak up some of my power. She had never done it before. I had become a tutelary deity whose foibles would be understood and pardoned from now on.

It was only when we reached home, only when I stood on my bed trying to hammer a nail into the wall without taking lumps out of the plaster that my folly caught up with me. A thousand dollars! It would have insulated us from the world for five years. And Julia? She never had any toys, except for a ten-year-old rabbit with an ear and a tail missing. I had to go to the bathroom to hide my tears from her. And then to bed with a bottle of Zubrowka to hide from myself.

That's when the mask struck.

I hear the roar of turbulent waters. There must be an immense waterfall near by. A band of naked black warriors stare at me with yellow eyes. They are standing in a circle, holding hands. I can hear the delicate rattle of the shells hanging from their necks. They murmur excitedly when I sit up. One of them approaches me slowly and gently palps my shoulder. His lower lip is pierced by a white tusk. He turns to the others: she is alive!

They rush to me like curious children, their cold fingers fondling my face, knees, breast and belly. They laugh and coo gently to one another. I want to rise but their fingers forbid it.

What are you doing to me? I implore the witch doctor. Why are you doing it?

Look! Look! he says to his companions. She has arrived!

'Wake up! Wake up! You're screaming, Mammy!' Julia tugged at me.

It took me a few minutes to shake off the warriors and the roaring of the waters. I felt cheated. But of what? By whom? I couldn't be sure. I went to the kitchen and brewed a mixture of valerian, sage and mint to calm my mind. I tried to brush it aside: odd what the excitement of the day and the claustrophobia of the last year could stir up!

But a part of me remained anxious and unconvinced, unpacified by the valerian and sage.

♦

'We have a problem, I'm afraid,' said Mrs Ursula Dembska leaning over her high desk with false concern. 'It's over to you now.'

Adventure Fourteen

(Who in the name of God is Ursula Dembska?)
(Wait till you see. She fits.)

She stared at me as if trying to decide whether I was all there. I understood then how weasels could hypnotize rabbits.

I wasn't all there. I could hardly follow what she was saying. I was staring back at her with sleepy eyes, waiting for my soul to return from the Congo.

'I'm sorry,' I said. 'What do you want me to do?'

'Talk to Julia. Explain the necessity of discipline in class. And of a bit more humility. As a psychologist you know better than I . . . '

'But what exactly is the problem?'

She threw up her ugly hands.

'I've been telling you for the last half an hour. None of her teachers can cope with her answers in class any more! Yesterday, for example, the biology master asked her how many legs a spider has. You know what she answered? She said: "Don't you have anything else to worry about?" And much the same in geography. When asked to list four African animals she replied: "One elephant and three giraffes." Now it's enough for her to stand up in class and the pupils fall over the place before she even opens her mouth! It's very demoralizing. As a psychologist you must know.'

On another day, after a good night's sleep, I would have been amused by Julia's impertinence. But my zebra dreams had drained all my energy.

'I'll talk to her,' I said, with my head in a fog.

'I know she's been through a difficult time,' Mrs Dembska went on, 'but it's over now and she has to adapt. She can't go on looking with contempt at other children, or indeed their teachers for that matter, because they haven't been in jail . . . It looks like jailbirds are the new aristocracy in this country,' she taunted, looking at me over the top of her glasses.

So I went home and told Julia to pretend that she was sane and normal for another year.

'I have to pretend at my Institute and I don't see why you shouldn't. Do it for me,' I said. 'I'm a very tired woman. I have to fight the secret police, the students at my Institute and the black men in Africa. Give me a break.'

'But it won't be the truth,' she protested.

'The truth will be a secret between us.'

I privatized the truth but I couldn't privatize my dreams. The warriors continued to carry me towards the sound of the roaring water. I could see the whitish insteps and heels of those who pranced and swaggered in front of the litter. They intoned a low mesmeric chant. A-li-a! A-li-a! and shook their spears in time to it. I struggled to rise but my limbs remained inert.

A-li-a! A-li-a!

I took down the zebra from over my bed but the dreams went on. I was a victim, an object, an initiate in some never-ending ritual. Waking up was no solace. I dreaded the day. There too I was a victim, an object, a toy in the hands of others.

Awake or asleep I was the plaything of some force beyond me.

Perhaps I was living two simultaneous lives in two hearts of darkness: one in General Jaruzelski's Kraków, the other with the Balubas on the banks of the Ubangi? And perhaps there was a third?

(Among the Fomorians in the west of Ireland?)
(Fomorians?)
However many lives, I'd rather not know about them.

One morning, over breakfast, when I was again waiting for my soul to return from the Congo, Julia stuck a Solidarity Bulletin under my nose.

'Look! The zebra man!'

There was a picture of the American we had met in the market. Peter Koltzov, leading American writer, gives $200,000 for Agricultural Foundation.

I had read some of Peter Koltzov's travel books. He specialized in describing bloody revolutions in unimportant countries. Wherever there was a coup, a putsch, an insurrection, a massacre, a peasant rebellion in the mountains, he arrived with the minimum of equipment and the maximum number of contacts. He was, as the tired blurbs claimed, a connoisseur of chaos. His books recorded with cool, surgical precision the atrocities and perversions of derailed humanity in remote places.

Clearly the mask was destined for him and not for me and Julia.

I rang Cezary. I rang him because he was mad and I could see that my case bordered on the end of psychology and the beginning of metaphysics.

'How wonderful,' he lisped. 'Evewybody's winging me these days. The whole city's going mad and wants me to explain why.'

'You were ahead of your time, Cezary. The rest of us are only catching up with you.'

Cezary went mad at a seance at which a group of Russian convicts interned deep in a Siberian mine had broken through to him. They had transcended their agony, risen above their own and others' bestialities, and were dying in bliss.

'Well, in your case it's clear that the Afwican mask is causing the disturbance,' he said. 'It will always dwaw your astwal body to the twibe where it belongs. The black men have twemendous power over you whether you want it or not. You must get wid of the thing.'

'What should I do? Burn it?'

'Oh God, no! Don't destwoy it whatever you do! You have to bwing it to where its power will be neutralized. To the Wawel perhaps. Yes, bwing it to the Wawel Cathedwal and leave it there in some cwack or cwanny. The black stone will do the job. For heaven's sake don't pass it on to anybody else.'

So when Julia was at school, pretending to be normal, I did the opposite. I wrapped the mask in a newspaper and carried it to the Wawel Cathedral. I didn't believe in the neutralizing power of ancient sites or black stones. And yet there I was, surreptitiously stuffing a magic mask behind the statue of I don't know what saint or martyr.

I walked back along the Vistula in a state of open revolt against myself. I had refused to sell the mask in the name of some higher principle which then turned against me and bit me. And how infantile of me to believe that I could lock up my nightmares in the Wawel!

I could hear the steps of the black warriors pounding after me.

A-li-a! A-li-a!

I didn't dare look back. A hand fell on my shoulder.

'Is this your package, missus?'

An altar boy in white surplice and red cassock looked at me suspiciously.

'I thought I saw you with it in the church.'

I wanted to give him a kick in the shins.

'Oh yes,' I said, gritting my teeth. 'Thank you for your trouble.'

I did the mask the honour of unwrapping it before carrying out the execution. Then, like a vestal with a wreath on

St John's Eve, I bore it to the edge of the river and flung it as far as I could into the Vistula.

Get Thee behind me, Satan!

I didn't look back in case the zebra was swimming against the current.

In my dreams I wandered once more where primordial horsetails and club mosses swayed nerveless tender arms above me. I returned to normal.

Now at last I was able to tolerate the cauchemars of the day, the interminable search for food, the secret police constantly at my heels and the threat of losing my job if I showed the slightest sign of insubordination.

My relief was the effect of stepping down from higher abnormality to lower abnormality. Like most citizens of the People's Republic, I had become an existential fakir. I could sleep on a bed of thorns because I was made to endure a bed of nails.

(You're beginning to sound like your great-grandmother.)

Adventure Fifteen

In which Faustyna Fast-forwards her Life

I rehearsed the predestined meeting with Peter Koltzov in my head, trying out various scenarios.

He calls one day to view the mask.

I drowned it, I say.

He swears and stomps out in a fury.

I meet him on the street and he asks casually, by the way, what about the mask?

I tell him I dedicated it as a votive offering to the Vistula.

In advance I check words like 'dedicated', 'votive' and 'offering' in the dictionary.

He thinks I'm mad.

One day he stands at the door with the zebra head in his hands.

He smiles.

I faint.

I knew the minute I saw him at the door, grinning and apologizing for his intrusion, that he had come to see me and not the mask.

'I don't have it any more. I threw it into the river.'

'You threw out the mask? Why?'

'Because it terrorized me.'

His face acquired a hawkish aspect, eyes shining, head inclined, nostrils flared.

'Tell me about it.'

So we sat down on the couch and drank elderberry tea and I stumbled and gesticulated through my tale.

He was captivated.

'Great stuff! Terrific! I wanted the mask but now you've given me something so much more valuable: a story about a mask. Or perhaps it's not for sale either?'

'I don't sell stories.' I said. 'You do.'

He beamed.

'You mean you know my stuff? What have you read?'

'Why are you here? There's almost nothing going on,' I circumvented his question.

'Nothing going on? I thought you people were falling to pieces.'

'But surely you are after something more . . . more brutal?'

'You mean life here is not brutal enough for you?' he smiled again.

I didn't know what to say.

'Why don't we talk it out over dinner? Friday night OK?'

He took out his diary.

'No, hold on. Friday I'm dining with the Cardinal. Saturday?'

'Sorry, Saturday I'm dining with Julia and her cat.'

The Cardinal riled me. And the diary riled me even more.

We agreed to meet on Wednesday at the Wierzynek. In those days it specialized in delicacies to tease the palates and pockets of the red bourgeoisie and Western tourists of the revolution.

The entry to the Wierzynek, as every entry to Paradise, was booby-trapped with trials and taboos. In the vestibule the Guardian of the Threshold challenged us with: There are no tables. The restaurant is full.

Of course, said Peter Koltzov and handed over a five dollar boon.

The ogress in reception said: I must see your identification.

Certainly, said Peter Koltzov and folded an offering into his passport.

A very sublime Master of the Inner Chamber challenged us on the first landing. I regret you will have to wait an hour, sir.

Naturally, said Peter Koltzov, discreetly stuffing a large ransom into the Master's waistcoat. We'd like the back room to ourselves, OK?

The Master called his minions, who escorted us to an empire table supported by caryatids.

Peter Koltzov didn't even glance at the scroll presented by the cupbearer. He flashed a green fetish with a pyramid and God's Eye inscribed on it and muttered: A bottle of rye vodka for starters and then Mouton Cadet 1973. Three bottles.

Thus faultlessly, under the coffered ceiling, we accomplished the Lesser Mysteries. Then began the Greater.

Above our table the kings of Europe and their dogs circa 1364 were feasting at the Great Conference of Monarchs. Casimir the Great, King Louis of Hungary, Waldemar, King of Denmark, the King of Cyprus, Princes of Austria and Pomerania and Margraves of Brandenburg ate and drank together unaware as yet that the greed and stupidity of their descendants would bring a continent to ruin.

And beneath them sat Peter Koltzov and I, unaware as yet that over the next three hours we were to live through a three-year love affair. It was as if we both pressed the fast-forward button on our lives so that we accelerated from seduction to courtship, from courtship to infatuation, from infatuation to domesticity, from domesticity to disagreement, from disagreement to divorce, all in the space of a single meal.

It was a dinner and a life in six courses.

APERITIF

Said Peter Koltzov, smacking his tongue. Somehow rye vodka tastes different in Kraków. Like fresh mangoes in Mauritius or draught Guinness in Dublin. Each thing is most piquant in its own place.

Do you think it's the same with people? I asked.

It depends. You see, when I go to a country I like to drink it, eat it, smell it and make love to it. That's the best way to get to know a place.

Is that why I'm here?

He smiled.

I'd like to know more about you. Faustyna – is it Faustyna as in Dr Faustus? Didn't he hang out here for a while studying alchemy or some such?

You will be disappointed. It's Faustyna as in Sister Faustyna. She was a Polish nun. Very holy. She saved my father's life.

Are you a Christian?

No.

Jewish?

I believe in Jehovah and that he is mad and bad. Very capricious. He loves you or rejects you for no reason. A kind of Stalin in the sky. He has his favourite peoples too.

The Poles are hardly one of them, smiled Peter Koltzov.

And what do you do, Faustyna?

I bear it.

I mean, what do you do for a living?

I panicked. The last ten years broke over me. How was I to translate into his language the brutal idiom of bottom-ification and betrayal?

The devil Frant, patron of lies, came to my rescue. The zebra trotting in my tipsy head led me on.

I work in the zoo, I said, intending a metaphor.

He was, as I hoped, taken aback.

Really, And what do you do in the zoo?

You know, I take care of giraffes and gryphons and so on . . .

After the fourth vodka I could see myself in wellingtons and overalls hosing down the elephants on hot days or throwing herrings to the seals. The place stank of gryphon dung. Now I could go on for ever.

The pelicans are my favourite. After them the armadillos.

Why armadillos?

I like the name.

What I don't understand is how you can keep a zoo when there isn't enough food to go around for the people.

You know how it is. Everybody adapts. People, animals adapt. The lions, for example, begin to be vegetarian. They eat potatoes.

He let me plunge on through my fiction as if he believed it all. The more lies I told the more he thrived on them. He even helped me to elaborate, prompting me with names and origins, genus and species.

We grew skittish and our eyes caught fire from one another.

He was letting me run loose to see if I was worth seducing.

I was.

◊

Adventure Fifteen

Adventure Fifteen

HORS-D'ŒUVRE: DALMATIAN SMOKED EELS WITH RUSSIAN CAVIAR AND CAPERS

My life in the zoo was as nothing compared to the stunning biography of Peter Koltzov. I regretted my own tendency to use up all my ammunition in the first salvoes and to leave myself empty and spent before an assailant. I had nothing left to throw at him and the vodka was beginning to flush my cheeks and fluster my brain.

Said Peter Koltzov. You seem pretty settled on the whole. Lucky you. I can't live a normal life. After a week of peaceful domesticity I have a breakdown. When I see myself in the bathroom mirror surrounded by porcelain and marble and polished chrome, you know, whistle-clean, bacteria-free surfaces, I ask that guy in the mirror, what are you doing here? So I open the newspaper and look for a war somewhere or a rumpus of some sort. And I go to my editor and I say, Larry, send me there.

Peter Koltzov had experienced everything. He had been arrested and beaten almost everywhere he went. He had faced his own death twice. He had been necklaced in South Africa and rescued at the last moment with the smell of burning rubber in his nostrils. He had stood before a firing squad in Cambodia and had been reprieved seconds before the order to shoot was given.

What thoughts did you have at these moments?
He smiled.

All that stuff about visions and past-life recall, is that what you mean? It's bullshit. All I could think of was how stupid it was to die like this, how quickly can we get it over with. Try some more vodka. A fish likes to swim, as you say here.

His stories ran long supple fingers down my back. Sun-drenched days in the hills of Sumatra kissed me between the eyes. I yielded to his bandaged head in San Salvador. Oh, how I yielded, how I cradled his broken body while he went on about the Chinese Book of Changes, Shahs of Iran, pygmy rituals, mad mullahs, sex in Samoa, Belfast brigades, Russian mystics, lamas and the stench of yak butter in Tibet.

CHANTERELLE SOUP WITH BISON BALLS

Said Peter Koltzov. Let me take you to my favourite place. It's a place not many people know about.

He lowered his voice and leaned forward. He had the conspiratorial look of a man about to divulge a secret.

We're in the west of Ireland. We're crossing Galway Bay. We're taking a hooker, a big black-bellied cow of a boat with a lateen sail. It's a bit romantic, a bit twee. We could have gone there by car or bus but, well, the adventure demands that we travel by boat. We're heading for a little harbour called Kinvara.

There's a grey Norman Tower House surrounded by a

bawn. And behind the village the low luminous hills of the Burren. How to put it? There's an ephemeral, lunar greyness in the air. You'd love it.

I'm not looking at Kinvara, wherever that is. I'm looking at Peter looking at Kinvara.

Said Peter Koltzov. People think that the springs of romance have dried up in Europe. That there are no more privileged places left where magical events can happen. The Burren is still such a place. *Na zdrowie.*

Cheers.

Everything is contradictory here, even the flora. There are Arctic mountain avens side by side with Mediterranean orchids. Things that shouldn't grow by the sea are growing down to the shore's edge. Plants that love forest cover are flourishing where there isn't a tree to be seen. What looks from a distance like a stone pavement is actually a fertile meadow rich with herbs. And there are herds of wild goats, like tribes of Indians, moving stealthily among the rocks.

And what do we do there?

We are in search of . . .

I never learned what we were searching for. The waiter came with the next course.

◊

MECKLENBURG ROAST GOOSE WITH REDCURRANTS, SULTANAS, CINNAMON AND BAKED APPLES

I didn't know you liked peaceful places. I thought you only liked revolutions. Blood in the streets, and so on.

Said Peter Koltzov. The goose is a little dry, don't you think?

Revolutions are a strange kind of drug. They keep you outside yourself. So then, well, you need to find yourself again. You need a place like the Burren. It's like a meditation. It detoxifies the mind. When you're in those violent God-forsaken holes in South America or wherever, the savagery clings to you like a bad smell. You need a desert or a high mountain to cleanse yourself.

The wise-man, Buddhist smile disappeared from his face. Peter Koltzov, the penultimate romantic, was leading me into the sanctuary of himself.

Said he. You know you're a very desirable woman. You make me see things in a new way. You make things strange. I haven't felt that way for a long time.

But I don't say anything.

Honey, it's the unsaid that stimulates.

I wondered what else I could keep silent about. But he wasn't very much interested in finding out. We were halfway through the second bottle of Mouton Cadet.

Proposed Peter Koltzov. Hey, listen up, what do you say to a trip to Texas? What do you say to a ranch with wild turkeys and deer, eh? I mean it. Your little girl would love it. We'd all go to the rodeos together and the rattlesnake-bagging festival.

So we settled on his ranch. A Swedish-style wooden mansion, lots of rooms, surrounded by live oaks and pecan trees. There was a creek just behind the house with a big pool for swimming in and lots of catfish. The extraterrestrials were watching Peter, Julia and me in sneakers and blue jeans walking among the cacti with bags full of squirming rattlesnakes.

I'll never get a passport.

Said Peter Koltzov. Come on. I'll fix it. They're eating from my hand after I helped prop up the Agricultural Bank.

May I ask you why you did it?

Because I believe that this country has a chance.

The chance to do what?

Said Peter Koltzov. All it needs is to have the pump primed. If you can manage to hold your course and not go berserk. If you manage to maintain the business of self-limiting revolution you guys could really make it. *Said he.* Don't look at me like that. All the revolutions and rebellions I've seen up to now got out of control and turned to savagery. You've managed to avoid it. *Said he.* You're still looking at me like that. You've come so far you mustn't spoil it at the last moment.

I flinched.

Said he. I know you may not like what I'm saying but I think you should trust your government. *Said he.* You may disagree with me but I believe that history will vindicate the General. He needs all the help he can get. For God's sake, after fifty years you're not going to go for capitalism, are you?

Said I. Oh shit.

Our idyll at the Texas ranch came to an abrupt end.

DESSERT: ROYAL MAZUREK *FOR ME AND* MAKOWKI *IN GRAND MARNIER FOR HIM*

(MacCoofky? Is that Scottish?)

(It's a poppy-seed cake, silly.)

The ultrasound from the Mouton Cadet was humming in my head.

I think it's stupid what you're doing. You're giving blood transfusions to a corpse.

Oh yeah? He was mashing his poppy-seed cake in the Grand Marnier and smiling indulgently. He had heard it all before.

The West has always made the same mistake. It's been financing slavery since the Second World War.

Oh yeah?

My rally over dessert took both of us by surprise. But I was so disappointed, so embittered by his stupidity that I had to have my say. I was zigzagging through my brain looking for the right words.

You're not supporting us with your dollars. You're supporting your own . . . your own romance!

He patiently removed a clot of whipped cream that I had splattered on the lapel of his jacket with my over-excited fork.

Come on, Faustyna, chill out.

The royal *mazurek* and the *makowki* made the silence endurable. This is how it would be on the ranch when Peter returned from the slaughter in Gambia or Zambia with his socialism intact.

Said he. Let's not quarrel. Let's have fun. What would you like to drink? Coffee and brandy?

No, I said, reverting to type. I'd like *miod*.

MIOD KASZTELANSKI *FOR ME AND CAPPUCCINO AND HENNESSY FOR HIM*

I was right. Peter Koltzov was investing in Peter Koltzov. He ignored me. He talked about himself. As he talked his face gradually changed shape and texture. He had written six books and five were international bestsellers. He didn't understand why. He was just a simple guy from Montana.

The pupils of his eyes were beginning to glow red. He liked simple people. If he had a mission in life, and it seemed he had, it was to defend the simple guy and express his authenticity.

The eye teeth were longer than they should have been. And sharper. Two of the books were made into films and three others were pending. It all meant more money than he knew what to do with.

The nostrils twitched. They had found the scent. He wasn't really interested in money. After all, he lived out of a suitcase. So he threw tens of thousands to foundations that looked after the little guys of this world.

He leaned across the table. His breath had the tangy odour of fresh blood.

Let me tell you something. The more I give the stuff away the more I get back. Jesus H. Christ knew something about investment when he told the little guy to cast his bread on the water. Let's drink to the little guys.

I raised my glass reluctantly. I had been completely upstaged by the little guys. They were the salt of the earth. Warm and human. No shit, if you'll excuse the expression, ma'am.

Had he brought them on to show up my pretentiousness and lack of authenticity?

Certainly his cheeks had a distinct Transylvanian pallor. Revulsion grew in me. How could somebody so self-absorbed, so preoccupied with his own importance, enter the lives of others? How could Peter Koltzov possibly write about me, for example. He hardly registered my presence. How could he ever reach the peons in Paraguay through his megalomania?

He liked to read his books to patients in cancer wards and hospices for the dying. He did it for free, though normally his agent could get him $2,000 a go at a university. Maybe I misunderstood. Maybe it was $3,000.

I was thinking about a cousin of mine who visited her dying brother in Pszczyna. As she left she said to him: Life is terrible. By the time I get home to Jastrzebie on my bike you'll be dead and mother will will have fallen into the fire. How will I manage?

Do you have to read books about dying to dying people? I said louder than necessary.

Said Peter K. with a knowing grin. There are no deaths in Peter Koltzov. There are only descriptions of death. It makes all the difference to the dying.

You mean death is a bourgeois invention?

Eagerly he misunderstood me.

Death is a story that gives shape and definition to life. People need a story as they near their own end. You wouldn't believe how grateful the patients were for the few hours I spent with them. They knew what I was talking about.

Our marriage was coming apart at the seams. I was determined to fight to the end. No quiet, self-effacing Texan housewife I. I had come to the point that when I hear *banialukas* I call them *banialukas*.

I opened my mouth. I wanted to say: *Dureń.*

(Dureń?)

(*Idiot, fool, piss-artist.*)

I opened my mouth but nothing came out. The words festered in my chest. They were in Polish to the point of pain and resisted translation. Not for the first time I wished we had been colonized by a less barbarous empire.

(*Like the English you mean?*)

(*Like the English.*)

(At least we would have a decent second tongue with which to quarrel with the world.)

I took a deep breath and calmed the glass of *miod* in my shaking hand. I was overreacting. (But then what woman wouldn't overreact if after three years she discovered that what she took to be the glow of her man's soul was only the faint iridescence of dead timber?)

It wasn't three years. It was three hours that I had been with the lout.

(The lout?)

(OK, he wasn't a lout. I was overreacting.)

I stood up abruptly, overturning the chair. I shook the crumbs off my dress the way the Apostles were told to shake the dust off their sandals.

Hey, what's going on? asked Peter Koltzov, puzzled. You ain't a million laughs, you know.

I was swaying from side to side like a blues singer.

I'm going home, I stammered.

He shook his head, smiled and finished off his brandy.

I'm going back to my own country.

I reckon you've spent too much time in that zoo of yours. I reckon the gryphons got to you in the end.

He won of course. I went back to the trivial boring horrors from which there was no escape. He went back to the spectacular horrors of his own choosing which gave him the feeling of being alive.

He was doubly the winner because he supported only the noblest cause, whatever the price.

Adventure Sixteen

In which Faustyna Meets an Angry Old Man

I'll finish soon.

My great-grandmother said: Most priests get ordained for the wrong reason. It's only afterwards they discover the right reason. Most people get married for the wrong reason. Years later the lucky ones invent the right reason.

Great-grandmother was a wise woman. She had stumbled on the Principle of Delayed Justification.

It took me a long time to invent my own reason for leaving the People's Republic.

I tried a myth: Bissula from conquered Swabia betrays her tribe and becomes a citizen of Rome because the imperial city enlarges her soul.

I tried psychology: one can keep up the internal pressure only for so long before the walls cave in.

I tried to follow the Great Man's advice.

Like all wise counsel at the time, it was given to me in church.

It was Holy Thursday. He sat in the third row on the side aisle, pretending to pray. Or maybe he really was praying, like all of them. I sat behind him in the fourth row and passed him my questionnaire folded into a Mass Book.

I was one of the very few to be granted the privilege of meeting the Great Man. I stared in awe at the back of his head, at the pink pancake of his bald skull surrounded by fluffy white hair.

The nave of the Mariacki Church was filling up with streams and tributaries of penitents. They swelled round the confessionals and flowed down the main aisle to where Suffering Jesus lay stretched on his cross. They queued patiently to unburden themselves of their sins and to kiss the body of the Redeemer, just as they queued for pork sausages and soap.

'Am I supposed to answer all these questions?' whispered the Great Man at last without moving his head.

'Yes.'

'And you mean to tell me that the others answered?'

'Yes. Well, not all of them, of course.'

'Don't talk to me directly,' he said sharply. 'Kneel down and speak into your joined hands.'

'I'm sorry.'

He sighed. 'Let's have another look. "One: Which do you prefer in the present situation? (a) A national uprising? (b) A guerrilla campaign? (c) A dialogue with the government." Are the people who sent you here out of their fucking minds?'

Even the candle flames before the Virgin Mary seemed to wither at the sound of the ugly word.

'We're simply trying to get a sense of what people want in the present situation,' I said too loudly.

'Calm down. I'll tell you what they want. (a) A cup of decent coffee. (b) A pair of cotton knickers. (c) A home where they can fuck without their granny hearing them in the next room.'

He was trying to prove that he was still a man or else to break the spell of *regnum et sacerdotum* that hung around us. But he was hunched and shrunken and his hair was thinning before my eyes. Soon the police will find him, he will spend a few years in jail, he will be released with the others, he will die of a heart attack before the nightmare ends.

'The last one I talked to wanted an American invasion as well,' I whispered.

I could hear a low chuckle.

'My dear girl, let's be honest. Your questionnaire is all balls. There's nothing to prefer. We have no guns and the government won't talk to us. You might just as well ask the mothers of Ethiopia which perfume they prefer: (a) Chanel or (b) Dior.'

I began to hate the flaky back of his head. I wanted to face him, to see what lay behind his jeers.

'The questionnaire may well seem idiotic to you. Yet it does reveal something. You know, we don't have much paper to . . . '

'Lower your voice, please.'

'To throw around. Sometimes I get a whole group of workers answering on the same sheet. And the thing is

205

that the group answers are always much less radical than the individual ones.'

'And so?'

'Well, this means that Solidarity has a moderating influence rather than a radicalizing one. It's rubbish to say that we've gone too far.'

He turned and looked at me for a brief second. I caught a glimpse of an Apostle from a Russian icon. St James? St John? St Peter, if it wasn't for the foul tongue.

'Maybe the commies should subsidize us? Tell me, why waste your time on this kind of investigation?'

'I thought I told you.'

'I can see that you've got a head on your shoulders. All these inane questions about how far and how long, where we should go and where we should stop – you must know it's nonsense as long as the real problem is not discussed.'

'And what's the real problem if you please, sir?'

'Go for the Leviathan. Study the Russians.'

I coughed.

'Why does everybody cough every time the Russians are mentioned? Why study our own impotence? Know your enemy. Study the colonizer, not the colonized.'

'If I'm not mistaken it's our own tanks that are in the street and not the Red Army's.'

'What?'

'Well it's our own tanks and not . . . ' I was blushing like a schoolgirl caught cheating.

'Don't add to the obligatory fantasy. In ten years' time all the political analysis on this country won't be worth a sparrow's fart. They'll think it as metaphysical as nineteenth-century theosophy.'

In the silence I could hear the shuffling of feet on their way to kiss the Cross.

(Isn't that a bit overdetermined? The Crucified Nation and all that?)

(Well, I can't help it. That's how it was.)

The Great Man rose and moved towards the aisle. I stood up as well, which I shouldn't have done, and followed him.

'Wait a minute! This work you suggest . . . I can't do it here.'

'Then get out of here,' he said through his teeth. 'And get back to your prayers, for Christ's sake.'

The faithful were kissing the crucified Christ. The shy ones embraced his feet. The more daring made for his head. Shameless women kissed all five wounds.

♦

Study the Russians! The Night of the Buttocks returned to haunt me. Mikhail Sergeyevich's impish eyes winked at me across the windy versts of Ukraine. It had taken fifteen years for his sluggish seed to sprout in me. What a crop of heresies it would yield!

And so it was that while everybody pissed on the present and future and gorged themselves on historical romances about the days when the Kingdom of the Two Nations stretched from the Baltic to the Black Sea I went baldheaded for the Russians.

The bookshops sold only the collected works of revolutionary prophets and the libraries were tightly controlled. I had to piece together my own secret collection from the Marquise de Custine to Zinoviev.

It was an archive of grief. My makeshift shelves sagged under the weight of pain that is Russia. Study the enemy! How could an empire built on such misery and chaos ever subjugate anybody? What kind of enemy yielded a Mater Dolorosa who cried

> *Mountains bow beneath that boundless sorrow,*
> *And the mighty river stops its flow.*
> *And those prison bolts are tried and thorough,*
> *And beyond them, every convict's burrow*
> *Tells a tale of mortal woe.*

We, by comparison, endured a kitchy, amateur agony. We said: Our situation is hopeless but not serious. We were comedians, in spite of all the suicides and tragic gestures. We were the parrot and the peacock of nations.

None of these justifications made much sense to me when I stood with Julia outside the Norwegian Embassy clutching our passports in which the police had stamped THE HOLDER IS ENTITLED TO LEAVE POLAND WITHOUT THE RIGHT TO RE-ENTER.

It would be an exaggeration to say that we were thrown out. On the other hand, our presence was no longer desired.

One day I was called to the police station. They had all seen *The Godfather*. They wanted to make me an offer I couldn't refuse.

What's the offer?

A passport. Choose your country. And get out.

It was that simple in the end. There were no stagey acts of rebellion to entertain you with, no rhetorical flourishes to quote for you now. No encountering for the millionth time the reality of experience to forge the conscience of my race or whatever it was the man said. Just fatigue.

(That's hardly like you.)

(All my life I've hardly been like me.)

(You left without a thought, then?)

I wondered about one thing on my way home. What would happen, I wondered, if every government got rid of its unwanted citizens in this way? The United Nations would have to establish (in Connemara? in Terra del Fuego?) a special reservation for the dispossessed.

Epilogue

In which the Author Owes the Reader an Explanation

It's raining again. Faustyna would say: I've never seen a country that could absorb so much water. Where does it all go?

(Into the limestone, my dear. Into the cracks and crevices.)

The oystercatchers, in their black and white evening dress, are scurrying among the rocks on the shore. We're in for a week of it.

Another week of rain and Faustyna and I'll go mad.

I've looked over her adventures once more with a sense of misgiving. One or two sound a bit far-fetched. But then, as her tiresome great-grandmother would say: Truth is a luxury. For some of us lies are a necessity.

And I miss a sense of pattern, a mandala at the centre of so much happenstance. Why Faustyna and where does she lead to?

She consistently refused to talk about the mundane or to dwell on the down-to-earth detail. Only adventure interested her; all the rest was onanism or socialist realism. I could never imagine her flat, for example, though I'm sure that there was a pile of old newspapers under her bed. What kind of make-up did she use in those days? What style of dress?

Are there really such places as Pszczyna and Jastrzebie? Or were they just tongue-twisting fricatives thrown in to bamboozle me in the small hours?

Even Kraków meant different things to us. For me it was a holy city, the seventh chakra of the earth, a centre of secret wisdom. It was the school of Apollonius of Tyre, of Dr Faustus, of John Dee and the Kabalists.

To her all this was *banialukas*, meaning raimeish. She jeered at my mystical hobby, at the pendulum and dowsing rod and my quest for the sacred geography of the Burren. At the same time she approved of it. At least I was a true Irishman with a spiritual aberration. Not like the other coons. Coons she had picked up from an Australian in Oxford.

I had to drag the bits and pieces of the *urbs sacra* out of her and she could never be sure if she hadn't mixed it all up. I've no way of knowing. I've never been to Kraków.

And finally the greatest difficulty. At first I tried to write it all down in the third person, a story about a woman called Faustyna: she said, she went and so on. But it wouldn't work like that. She demanded to speak in her own voice without any beating round the bush. She was shameless in her malice and her desire to outshine me. In the end I had to let her have her own way. So as well as being her seventh lover (by my count) I became her midwife too.

Shelley (or maybe it was Keats?) kept rotten apples on

his desk to incite him to write when his inspiration flagged. I keep a multichannel Hitachi radio. When I can no longer hear in my head that thick Slavic accent of hers with its recurring snorts as of a bagpipe taking air, I prowl the short wave for Radio Moscow or the English Language Service of Radio Bulgaria. Once I catch the timbre and texture of those wavering Eastern European voices looming out of the static I find Faustyna again, crouched over the turf fire, chain-smoking Marlboros, one hand in the folds of her flannel skirt.

I wonder now: was our meeting an insignificant episode in her life? Or would she account it an adventure and acclaim it with a capital A? Would she one day stretch out on somebody's sofa, blow a few preliminary smoke rings in the air and begin:

After Trondheim, after Oxford, when Julia was with her father in Mombasa, I felt I was drying out like an old baba. As we know, the English don't enjoy women very much. I was becoming invisible again, like in those horrible interrogation rooms in Kraków. Then I remembered Peter Koltzov seducing me among imaginary hills and holy wells in Ireland, his smile switched off at last. So one day I found myself standing with a rented bicycle at the foot of a hill called something Mama.

Excuse me, but what is this Mama about? I asked the first man I met on the road.

He was younger than me but looked right for the place – the usual Irish freckles, unwashed hair and a face of exalted innocence.

Not Mama, he said, glancing shyly at my bosom. *Uacht Mauma*: the Cream of the Breast. Honey Hill.

That's enough. She wants to take over again and already she's telling lies.

Uacht Mauma, I said, not looking at her bosom but at the flat tyre on her bike. She confused me right enough. She looked Irish with her pale face and red hair but the abruptness of her question and her hard accent were from another world. And if I had an exalted look on my face it was because, compass in hand, I was following a ley line from Bishop's Quarter to Killmachduagh.

That evening I met her again on a green path huddled over a half-dismembered bicycle.

At last, she remonstrated. You took your time about coming back.

While I worked on the bike she sat on a stone wall, smoked, and fired questions at me. Was the IRA active in this part of the country? What did I think of the British presence? The Anglo-Irish Agreement – would it improve anything? Why was the country in such a mess?

I tried to draw her attention to the landscape but she had no interest in a heap of old stones she said. Why do people waste their time building so many walls for Christ's sake?

When she stretched out on the horsehair sofa in my cottage I marvelled at the way someone from God knows where, someone I'd never met before, could so completely take possession of my life. Perhaps I had spent too much time with places rather than people? I had taken refuge in the landscape and was then doubly fascinated by the human world of which she spoke so obsessively. Or maybe it was her foreignness that attracted me? Up till then I had just one Irish woman in my life – my mother – and that was enough for me.

There was something in Faustyna that made me attentive. Not her disquieting green eyes or her youthful face or her Marlene Dietrich legs. It was something that had crystallized in her a long time ago, before even the buttocky cloud and Mr Gorbachev's intervention. What was it?

My mind has been formed in the realms of lower probability, she jested.

I'm not at all sure I know what she meant.

She hadn't come to Ireland to detoxify herself *à la* Peter Koltzov, if indeed he ever existed. Her visit to Clare was incidental to her visit to Galway, where she had applied for a job at the university. She failed to get it. When I probed her for details she said enigmatically: I was interviewed by five males and none of them was a man.

Come on, I said, spell it out for me.

Despondently, chewing the grounds of her Turkish coffee, she spelled it out. Well, if I must know, one of them was uncomfortably tall and another uncomfortably small, with hard bright eyes and a twisted mouth that gulped all the available oxygen. The tall one kept leaving the room, ostentatiously, to take telephone calls from

Brussels. Maybe the poor man had a prostate problem? The small one spoke in dazzling paragraphs. He chuckled over his own jokes and paused only to admire his own brilliance. He reminded her of the so-called Minister for Disinformation at home whose brilliance was empowered by unremitting hatred. The other three sat cowed between the tall and the small, making mysterious notes on bits of paper. None of them looked her in the eye when she described her theory of the Patrimonial Pendulum and how it explained everything about Soviet society. They were monks on the inside and social scientists on the outside. Towards the end of the interview one of them asked her if she spoke Irish.

Maybe you should try the Regional College? I suggested.

No, she shot back, once was enough. The interview board was Ireland in miniature. An unappetizing mixture of gracelessness, brilliance and fear of women. Better Kraków under martial law than Galway under any circumstances.

She stayed a week with me in my cottage, rapidly turning the place into a chaos of books, newspapers and discarded coffee cups. Once or twice, as if stricken by the memory of her femininity, she spent the afternoon in the kitchen mixing honey, oats and lemon and plastering it on her face. Or she covered her head with a towel and held it over a bowl of steaming camomile. Don't pay attention to me, she pleaded. When I'm beautiful again I'll make you

Russian *pirogis* with mushrooms. But she forgot her promise in the fervour of her remembrance of things past.

Long past midnight we would collapse into our Kinvara clinch, a tight meditative embrace, all the sweeter because it came from nowhere and was going nowhere.

She refused to explore the countryside with me or go sightseeing. So I put aside my book on sacred geography and listened to her motley adventures and the *Dindshenchas* of Kraków.

(Dindshenchas?)

(The lore of high places.)

When she caught me taking notes surreptitiously she grinned and began to spell out names for me.

Nothing lasts for ever, nothing happens twice, she quoted her great-grandmother one last time on the morning she left. It was pointless to ask her her plans because she would either lie or give me one of her enigmatic replies. Like: I'm not going anywhere but I won't stay either.

I offered her a lift as far as Galway but she said no.

No, she said, I like to cycle on wet days. It's only on my bike I can cry as much as I want.

She looked at me with that insistent ironic gaze I had come to mistrust.

You see, I can pedal away and cry like a beaver and nobody can tell my tears from the rain.